CALLIE'S CA[

Mountain Men of Montana 2

Jane Jamison

MENAGE EVERLASTING

Siren Publishing, Inc.
www.SirenPublishing.com

A SIREN PUBLISHING BOOK
IMPRINT: Ménage Everlasting

CALLIE'S CAPTORS
Copyright © 2013 by Jane Jamison

ISBN: 978-1-62242-979-0

First Printing: April 2013

Cover design by Les Byerley
All art and logo copyright © 2013 by Siren Publishing, Inc.

Printed in the U.S.A.

PUBLISHER
Siren Publishing, Inc.
www.SirenPublishing.com

DEDICATION

Readers,

Thank you so much for your support. I appreciate the time you take to read my books. I hope you enjoy reading them as much as I enjoy writing them.

CALLIE'S CAPTORS

Mountain Men of Montana 2

JANE JAMISON
Copyright © 2013

Chapter One

The day had started out on a chilly note, but had swiftly warmed up. Considering she was in the mountains of Montana, Callie considered herself lucky that the weather was cooperating. Although it was springtime, things could change at a moment's notice. Late snowstorms could pop up, thrusting the woods from the warmth of spring back into winter. But she wasn't worried. Callie Kirkland prided herself on being prepared. Growing up in the foster care system of a large city had taught her independence and how to handle herself in all kinds of situations. She'd taken those urban skills and had adapted them to the outdoors.

She loved the forest best. But she adored every bit of Mother Nature's offerings from the beaches to the flat plains of the Midwest and on into the mountains located on both sides of the country. Maybe her love was a result of having lived in four different foster homes in Atlanta, each one chaotic and turbulent with shouting and fighting a constant factor. Or maybe it was simply in her genes. Since she knew nothing about either of her parents, it was anyone's guess.

She stepped over a log then stopped. The sound of running water told her a stream was close by, tempting her to dip her toes into the cool liquid. She shifted the backpack into a more comfortable position, then started toward the babbling noise.

The song "Running with the Moon" came to her lips as it often did whenever she was hiking. It wasn't something most twenty-five-year-olds might sing, but she'd liked it from the first time she'd heard it while cruising along the roadway in the beat-up older Jeep she'd purchased on her seventeenth birthday. She preferred driving at night and had felt a strange sense of longing to be a part of something more as she'd listened to the song and glanced up at the full moon hanging in the blue-black sky. It was as though the moon called to her, trying to tell her of a life that was different than the one she'd known.

"Let's go running with the moon. Running. Running away."

A breeze lifted her hair away from her shoulders as she continued to sing. Her voice grew stronger as the memory of how she'd sung it while hurrying around the kitchen of the popular Atlanta restaurant where she'd worked, underage and paid under the counter, came back to her. The work had been hard, but she'd managed to save her tips as a waitress until, at last, she'd accumulated enough cash to quit her job, ditch the small furnished apartment she'd rented since aging out of the system, and fulfill her dream of hitchhiking around the country. That was over a year ago, and along with taking a menial job every once in a while to supplement the income she made from her photography, she'd managed to keep herself fed and clothed.

Except for the gnawing in her gut telling her that she needed something more, life couldn't get much better.

A noise to her left brought her up short. She listened, using the heightened sense of hearing that she'd been blessed with from birth. Her friends had teased her about it, calling her "Radar" as a term of endearment.

The crackling of the leaves came again, and slowly, making as little noise as possible, she slid her backpack to the ground. She knelt and unzipped it then reached inside to find the camera that was always on top of everything else. A long, sharp knife rested directly below the camera, but she'd never had to use it for self-defense and hoped she never would.

The sound came again as she started to creep in that direction. Taking care to keep the branches from scratching her, she eased her way through the underbrush. She was closer and more noise, sounds that signaled the proximity of an animal, added to the mix. She could hear its breathing, the low grunts as it moved, and the bright splashing of water. Whatever was ahead was using the stream she wanted to enjoy.

She pushed through the next bush, then paused as a dark form took shape. She held her breath, enraptured by the sight of the animal. A large, ten-point buck stood in the water, letting the liquid flow over the lower half of its legs. He was huge, larger than any she'd ever seen. His body was muscled and toned, the dark of his fur spreading across his back and leading to the bushy, white-tipped tail that swished back and forth. His enormous antlers rose to the sky, the gray of them startling against the green backdrop of the forest. Snowy white surrounded his black nose then jumped over the dark brown along his shoulders to run the course of his belly. His chest had a streak of black running from his neck to his belly. He was, simply put, a magnificent animal to behold.

She clicked away, snapping photographs as fast as she could. Each frame was even better than the last. She smiled at him, silently thanking him for showing up to become the star of her work.

Big, black eyes fixed on her as he turned his head toward her. Yet she wasn't afraid. How could anyone be afraid of something so beautiful?

He snorted, dropping his head and pointing his antlers at her. The way he acted was unusually aggressive for a deer, but she was too involved in taking the photograph to be worried. Even then, she doubted he'd do anything more than bluster and stomp, splashing the water about in his attempt to frighten her away. It wasn't until he burst out of the water like a mass of energy exploding from confinement that she lowered her camera and gaped at him. Water sprayed everywhere, dotting his chest with shiny diamonds of water and making sparkling lights in the air.

Oh, shit!

She took off running, holding her camera in one hand as she used the other to break through the forest. He snorted, blowing air through his nose as he pounded toward her. When she glanced back, the sight of him gaining ground on her spurred her into running harder and she no longer felt the sting of the branches tearing at her skin.

Passing the spot where she'd left her backpack, she snatched up the backpack then started running again and didn't look back. He was so close she could almost feel the warmth of his breath on the back of her neck.

She couldn't think. She could only run.

Breaking into a clearing, she let out a small whimper, yet felt a flush of relief. He should've already caught up with her, but she didn't dare question her good luck. If only the luck would stay with her a little while longer, she might make it to the other side of the grassy area. Then, just maybe, she could hightail her butt up a tree far enough to stay clear of his deadly antlers.

Something hit her, washing over her as though she were trying to run through water. The instinct to survive took charge and she kept moving even though her vision blurred and she found it difficult to breathe. A dry heat cocooned her, at once supporting her yet making her unsteady on her feet. It was if she'd entered an invisible wind tunnel and was struggling to push through to the other end.

Her mind, clouded with alarm, couldn't make sense of the sensations rippling over her body. Instead, she struggled on, determined to make it to the end. Providing the strange area of wind had an end.

When at last she made it to the other side of the clearing, she broke out of the strange barrier and stumbled forward, thrown off balance by the sudden lack of resistance against her. Her backpack and camera went flying and, just as she started to pick them up, the buck appeared. With no other choice, she left her possessions and darted into the underbrush, not caring where she was going, only that she had to get away. The buck was only a few feet behind her, the steady rhythm of his hooves striking the dirt. With her breath catching in her throat and a stitch aching in her side, she kept going.

All at once, she was falling, tumbling in a downward spiral. She screamed and reached out for anything to break her fall, but could find nothing. She tumbled, fast and hard, until she landed on her back. The air rushed out of her, depriving her lungs and clenching the muscles in her chest. An ache barreled through the rest of her body, bulleting it with pain as she squinted her eyes closed. She hurt everywhere, and yet, at the same time, she was aware enough to realize that nothing was broken.

The buck's snort made her open her eyes, and when she did, she found herself gazing up at him. She was in a deep hole, a pit, but at least she was safe from the animal.

Callie lay still, letting her heart slow down and her breath even out. The buck pranced at the edge of the pit and stared down at her. His dark eyes met hers and blinked.

Groaning, she pulled her aching body into a sitting position and waited for any fresh pain to come. When none did, she glared at the animal, then pushed her body into a standing position. But standing proved harder than she thought and she had to rest against the dirt wall to keep on her feet.

The buck lowered his head then raked his hoof along the edge sending a powder of dirt drifting down on top of her. She yelped and moved out of the way.

"Get away from me. You're the reason I'm in this mess."

The buck blinked again, then continued to stare at her. Was he trying to understand her, or had her imagination gone as wild as her run?

"You're losing it, girl," she whispered.

She pulled her cell phone out of her back pocket and held it up, inspecting it for damage. "Please don't let it be broken." Yet, although the phone was intact and the home screen came on as it always did, she couldn't get any reception. She held it higher but still no bars.

"Damn it all." She paced to the other wall and ignored the animal when he started circling the hole. If she didn't get a call out, who knew how long she'd be trapped?

The buck snorted and shook his head.

"What is with you anyway? Why are you still here?" She really studied the animal then. "If I didn't know better, I'd say you ran me into this pit on purpose."

But that didn't make sense. Why would an animal that was known to be as docile as a deer suddenly want to hurt a human? Had her camera spooked him?

He snorted again and shook his head several times. After checking one more time, she shoved her phone back into her pocket then found a flat spot to sit on. The sun was heading westward and soon it would get dark. Although she'd prepared for every imaginable situation—or so she'd thought—she hadn't planned on falling into a hole. Especially after getting chased by a huge buck and without her backpack filled with necessary supplies.

"I don't suppose telling you to go for help would work." She let out a rueful chuckle. "Yeah, right. Like you're some kind of woodland Lassie."

She hugged her knees to her chest. One rule she'd never followed while hiking was to tell someone where she was headed. Besides, who was she supposed to tell when she had no one in her life?

A sudden rush of tears welled in her eyes. She wasn't a crier by nature, but if any time was a good time to cry, it was now. Letting go of her usually controlled emotions, she let the tears slide down her face. Sobs racked her body as she crossed her arms over her bent knees, laid her forehead on her arms, and gave in to her dismay. She stayed that way, huddled in the hole for an indeterminate amount of time.

The shadows of evening fell over her, drawing her attention upward. The buck was gone, and, although she knew it wasn't rational, she couldn't help but feel lonely. Now she really was alone. She waited for a while, hoping that maybe the buck would return, but when he didn't, she pulled herself together.

At least the moon's still there.

She could always count on the moon.

She was in a tough spot, but she'd been in tough spots before. After surviving an abusive foster mother who had then sent her packing to the next foster home and straight into the arms of a foster father who'd tried to rape her, getting caught in a hole seemed almost laughable. And not something that could beat her.

Drawing in a big breath, she went around the interior of the hole, checking for any indentations that she could use as a handhold. She'd rock climbed before, and although she'd had the necessary equipment for those treks, she had to believe that she could climb out of the hole, too.

"You can do this. No problem."

She took hold of a rock that jutted out from the wall and stuck the tip of her shoes into a smaller crevice below. Pulling her body up, she skimmed her hand along the surface, but couldn't find another rock to grab on to. Instead, she held on with one hand and started digging.

But the wall was harder than it looked. Instead of working her fingers into what she'd hoped was dirt, she could only swipe away a thin layer that covered a wall of rock. She tried another spot and found more rock. Groaning, she dropped back to the floor.

She couldn't dig handholds into that rock. Not without tools. But she didn't even have the right kind of tools in her pack. And her pack? She didn't even want to think about that.

She cried out as her backpack landed on the dirt beside her. A few inches closer and it would've hit her. She gaped at it, then twisted around to gawk at was above her. What she saw sent her stumbling backward.

"Holy hell."

A creature leaned on all fours, peering over the rim of the wall, perilously close to falling off. He had no fur covering his bone-thin black body. Bloodred eyes peered at her from a narrow oval face with two holes bored into the flesh that served as nostrils and a long, thin jaw. His front arms hung in front of him like a gorilla's did when walking. A diamond-shaped spot of white brightened his forehead.

It tilted its head as though trying to figure out what she was and why she was there. But when its mouth stretched wide to expose dagger-sharp fangs, she couldn't hold back a gasp. It wrinkled its forehead, giving its face a scrunched-up appearance and opening his nostrils wider. He reminded her of the drawings of aliens with their huge eyes and expressionless faces combined with the distorted combination body of a wolf mixed with a human.

Had it thrown her backpack to her? Or, more likely, dropped it? But why did it have her belongings anyway? She swallowed and waited for whatever would happen next.

Scrunch, as she suddenly named the creature, lifted his front paw in what, from a human, would've looked like a wave. Whether or not he was male was obvious when he lifted onto his back legs and exposed his erect cock. She widened her eyes then looked away. Would she encourage him by looking at it?

Damn, I hope not. I am not playing Jane to some alien-ape thing.

"Gwegun."

She jerked her head up again. "What? Did you say something?"

He tilted his head again, reminding her of the way a dog would when trying to understand its master. But was Scrunch the master or was she?

"Gwegun bles."

Curiosity made a fast track in overtaking her fear. "You did. You spoke." She took a step toward that side of the pit. "But I don't understand."

He pointed at her backpack and grunted several times. The lines of verbal communication were deteriorating. She squatted next to the bag. "Yeah. This is mine. Thanks for bringing it."

Rummaging through it relieved her anxiety a bit. Nothing was gone except for a couple of granola bars and her water bottle. Even her camera had been tucked securely inside it.

"I guess a couple of snack bars are a good price to pay to get my stuff back." She searched again, although she was sure she wouldn't find her water. "But you could've left me a little to drink considering I'm stuck down here."

She stood and he started hopping up and down on his front feet, his excitement brightening his red eyes. "Unless, of course, you can help me get out of here." But if he did, would she be safe with him? Or safer in the hole? Still, what choice did she have?

"Listen, Scrunch, can you help me out of this mess?" She smiled and was surprised to see him copy her gesture. At least she hoped it was a smile. "If you help me, I'll buy you a whole carton of granola bars. Even the gooey, bad-for-you chocolate ones. How about it?"

He scrunched up his face even more, giving him a strangely wizened expression. After a couple more grunts, however, she was sure he wasn't going to give her any help.

"Okay, so don't help. I've done just fine on my own." Until now.

She plopped down on the ground and resisted the urge to cry again. Scrunch lay down by the edge and stared at her. They stayed that way for a while as the moon floated across the sky.

Suddenly, he stiffened and jerked his head up. His gaze scanned the horizon on the other side of the hole. Every part of his body was ready to spring into action.

"What is it? What do you see?"

Scrunch brought out his fangs and hunkered down, digging long claws into the dirt. Saliva dripped from his teeth and any idea she'd had that he was docile was gone. She had no doubt he could tear her apart if he wanted.

She pivoted toward the direction of his attention even though it put her back to him. But the hole was too deep for her to see anything.

Another deeper, meaner growl rolled out of Scrunch. She glanced up just in time to see him dart away, moving faster than she'd have thought possible.

"Scrunch! No, don't leave. No one knows I'm here."

Did she expect him to call for help? It was a ridiculous idea, but, like when the buck had stood over her, having him around had made her feel better. She stared at the place where he'd been and wished for him to return.

Another growl had her spinning toward the sound. She gasped and flattened her body against the wall.

"Oh, holy hell. I am so screwed."

Chapter Two

Three huge wolves, their gazes hard and steellike, stared down at her. She hurried to her backpack and rummaged through it, hunting her knife. It wouldn't do much good if all three attacked her, but at least she'd go down with a fight. She found the knife then backed toward the side of the pit that was farthest from them.

Even though her heart pounded in her ears, she couldn't help but admire them. One was a golden color with shades of light brown covering his haunches. A white streak ran down his face to the end of his nose and tipped the ends of his ears. He stood like the other two, large paws planted apart as he swished his tail.

The one standing next to him had dark hair with lighter brown covering parts of his body then blending back into black before lightening again. He lacked the white accents and he was bigger, his chest wider than the first wolf's.

The third broke apart from the trio to pace a few feet away. His fur was coal black with no variation in his coloring, making him a striking contrast to the other two wolves.

They were beautiful and majestic, a sight anyone would appreciate. But it was their eyes, locked so intently on her, that took her breath away. The amber in them shone in the darkness, but it wasn't the color that had her gasping. Instead, it was the way they looked at her.

As she would've imagined, their eyes held a hunger. But she couldn't help but think their hunger was not born from a lack of physical nourishment. No, the hunger was one of longing, like a child's gaze when he presses his nose against a toy shop window and yearns for the bright, shiny toy beyond his reach.

The first wolf paced the other way and took a position at her back. Surrounded, she moved into the middle of the pit but again recognized the futility of any attempt to win if they decided to take her.

"Get out of here!" She held her knife up in what she hoped the animals would take as a threatening gesture. "Go on. Get! I'll cut you if you try to hurt me."

Were they grinning at her? She squinted, trying to see better even though a full moon spread its glow over the land.

Almost as if in challenge to her threat, the first wolf hunched down, then leapt across the hole to land next to his pack mate. She yelped, then hated herself for letting him scare her. Wasn't it a good sign that he hadn't jumped into the pit?

Her breathing hurt her throat as she dragged in air. She'd run across wild animals before and had either scared them off or gotten away from them. But this was different. She was vulnerable and caught in a trap with nowhere to run.

Still, she was surprised when the black wolf leapt into the hole and landed a few short feet away. Startled, she moved backward and stumbled over her backpack. She scrambled to her feet, taking her pack with her to hold in front of her.

For the first time ever, she wished she had a gun. But she'd never been able to stand the idea of shooting an animal.

The black wolf tilted his head at her as Scrunch had done. In fact, there were many similarities between Scrunch and the wolves. Almost bone-thin to the point of emaciation, Scrunch had resembled a wolf, albeit with a more human-like face. She shook her head, surprised that she could think of the strange creature while an attack was imminent. She prepared herself for the pain that would come with the first bite.

"Stay back." *Yeah, uh-huh. Like he'll do what I tell him to do.*

Instead, he lowered his head and inched forward. She clutched her pack to her chest and held out her knife. The wolf shook his head.

Was he answering her threat?

When he sat down on his haunches, she was left speechless. In a matter of seconds, he'd transformed from a wild beast to a friendly animal. She lowered her hand, but she still clutched the knife.

They stayed that way for several minutes, eyeing one another, sizing each other up. The black wolf watched her as the two other wolves moved around the hole. But she didn't sense any danger from them. Instead, they seemed as curious as she was.

"So we're okay? You're not going to eat me?"

He pulled back his lips. *Damn it all. It's not my imagination. He's smiling at me.*

She dropped her backpack and slid to the ground beside it. "I don't know if I believe this, but I'm going to take full advantage of it anyway."

Daring to put her knife on the ground, she pulled the flaps open and pulled out her camera. "At least if I'm going to end up as your dinner, there'll be photographic evidence." She lifted the camera and adjusted the settings. "Smile, big wolfie."

She almost forgot to push the button when he did just that. Biting her lower lip, she clicked off more photos. With each successive picture, he shortened the distance between them. She fought against the fear stiffening her spine, determined to not let him stop her. Before long, he was less than a foot from her.

The growl rumbling out of his throat threw her off her game. Dragging in a long breath, she lowered the camera and found herself staring into the amber eyes of the wolf.

"Oh, my God," she whispered.

* * * *

Pete Deacon couldn't take his eyes off her. She was the most beautiful woman he'd ever seen. Her eyes were big ovals that were locked onto his, in a face so sweet the sight of it would make the angels in heaven jealous. A sprinkling of freckles raced over the bridge of her nose, but that didn't lessen the sultriness of her pouty lips. Her long, black hair, as dark as his fur, hung in ringlets around her face, over her chest, and disappeared down her back. She was tanned by days spent in the sun and her lean body showed that she was in shape, yet curvaceous.

Her eyes were what lit his soul on fire. He could see fear in them, but beyond that, he saw courage and intelligence. She'd managed to stay calm after he'd jumped into the pit. Even now, when she should've been frightened out of her wits, she was composed enough that her hands didn't shake. Hopefully, that meant she wouldn't grab her knife and try to stab him.

A growl from his brother, Blue, interrupted his thoughts, but he didn't take his gaze from hers. Raine, his other brother, would be as anxious as Blue for him to get out of the hole and move into the forest where they could talk. But he wanted to linger not only to memorize every inch of her face, but to draw in her intoxicating scent. The aroma was a heady mix of the woods, sweat, and her own unusual, flowery scent. He could've stayed there forever and lived off her fragrance.

But Blue had other ideas. Growling again, he whirled around and dashed toward the woods. Raine danced on his feet, waiting for Pete to jump out of the hole, but when he didn't, he gave up and chased after Blue.

She glanced up, noted their departure, then lowered her eyes to his. Her lips parted and he had to resist the urge to shift back to human form so he could kiss them.

"Go."

It wasn't a command. Her whisper was a plea, but it held a tone of regret, too.

He had to leave. He knew his brothers were waiting for him. In his present form, there was nothing he could do for her anyway. But he couldn't leave before he did one thing first. Lifting his head higher, he reached out and slid his tongue along her cheek.

She jerked, but didn't scream or try to get away. Instead, she lifted her fingers and touched the spot where he'd licked her.

She tasted even better than she smelled.

A howl broke the silence of the night. He stepped away from her.

Damn you, Blue. Shut the hell up.

Gathering his strength, he crouched then hurled his body out of the pit. He spun around and looked back at her. She stood, her camera still in her hands, as he lifted his head and howled his answer to his waiting brothers. With a flick of his tail, he bolted and ran toward the woods.

Raine and Blue stood just past the edge of the trees, hidden by the dense foliage, but he could still find them easily enough. Since they were back in their human bodies, he shifted, too.

"How did she get in?" Blue's eyes, a testament to his name, glittered with excitement.

Although Raine shook his head, his own blue eyes blazing, he still gave an answer. "She has to be a werewolf."

Pete glanced back at the hole. "No, there has to be another answer. If she's a werewolf, why doesn't she shift and jump out?" He shook his head, mimicking his brother's gesture. "Could someone else have brought her into The Hidden?"

"And then desert her?" Blue sniffed the air. "If someone did, they ought to get strung up. I can still smell the stench of The Cursed."

Pete caught the scent, too, but at least the odor wasn't strong. That meant only one or two of the wretched creatures had been around. "If they saw her, then they'll tell the rest."

"You don't think one of them brought her through, do you?"

Pete cringed at Raine's question. "Let's hope not. If one of them dragged her inside, then that means they can get on The Outside now."

None of The Cursed aside from the leader Burac had ever been able to go to The Outside. And they'd had no indication that any of them could leave and return as Burac had done.

Since his death, the Cursed's attacks on the people of The Hidden had happened less frequently than before. A few had even said they'd run across The Cursed and had seen no aggression from them. But the past was difficult to forget and the people weren't ready to believe that The Cursed could change.

Blue's concentrated thought made creases in his forehead. "None of us is getting this right. We're missing something and the best way to figure out what that is would be to talk to her."

Pete grabbed Blue's arm to keep his brother from taking another step. "I agree, but don't you think we'd have better luck if we had some clothes on?"

As it often did, Raine's crooked grin preceded his joke. "That depends on what kind of luck we're wanting."

But they both knew he was right. As shifters often did in The Hidden, they'd left what few clothes they had back in their tent at camp. Their tent wasn't very large since they preferred to sleep in the woods at the edge of the community that served as home for all kinds of supernatural beings. Werewolves were the predominant form of shifter within their group, but The Hidden was also a refuge to fairies, werecats, werebears, and skinwalkers. The Deacon brothers often stayed in their wolf forms, running through the forest and howling at the moon.

"Okay, then, let's get our clothes."

"We can't leave her alone, Blue. What if The Cursed comes back?" Pete didn't want to risk that happening. "I'll stay here and keep watch. You two head back and grab our clothes. Once we're dressed, we can show our faces to her."

"Pete's right." Blue was the oldest, but he rarely asserted his authority. Raine was a couple of years younger at twenty-six and Pete a year younger than him at twenty-five years of age.

Pete was thirteen years old when Blue and Raine's parents had found him wandering the woods surrounding The Hidden. He'd been frightened and hungry, but he'd still tried to fight them by shifting into his wolf form and lunging at them, fangs bare, and claws extended. They'd easily subdued him, and after finding out that his mother had abandoned him, pushing him out of the car on a lonely mountain road, the Deacons had welcomed him into their lives and their family.

Pete's story wasn't an unusual one. Often, a human mother couldn't raise a werewolf child that had somehow transformed without becoming a full werewolf. Seeing their child shift was too hard, and soon, they'd find a way to be rid of them. Many of the children who hadn't changed yet ended up being raised by the human social services system while others, like Pete, were cast aside to fend for themselves.

Blue was good at solving problems and Pete envied his older adopted brother's quick and logical mind. "Good. Then like I said, I'll stick around and watch over her."

Raine shoved him. "Why do you get to stay? Haven't you always claimed to be the fastest runner? As such you and Blue can use your considerable speed and make it quicker than I ever could."

Pete wasn't falling for the flattery. How many times had Raine boasted that he could outrun them? "No thanks. Besides, I called it first. I'm sticking and you two are hoofing it. Now get going. I don't like the idea of hanging around here any longer than I have to."

Blue arched an eyebrow. "Hang on. Who knows when The Cursed might get back? I'll stay with you in case they do."

Raine narrowed his eyes, but he knew he'd been outmaneuvered. "Damn. I wish I'd thought of that. Fine. I'll go to the camp and fetch our clothes."

Pete hated it when Raine used canine references. But knowing that Raine had probably done it just to get on his nerves, he refrained from showing his irritation. Raine didn't mean any harm, he simply liked to joke. "Then get moving, bro."

Raine took a deep breath and looked longingly in the direction of the hole. "You guys promise not to do anything, even talk to her, until I get back?"

"We'll do what we have to do. Who can say what that will entail?"

Pete liked that Blue was ready to give Raine a taste of his own medicine. "Yeah. If we have to jump in and snatch her into our arms to keep her safe, then that's what we'll do. After all, someone's got to make the sacrifice."

Raine snorted his derision. "Some sacrifice. She's so hot I'm surprised steam isn't rising from there."

Pete could see the lust he felt on his brothers' faces. "She is that. Do you think she's taken?"

Unlike werewolves outside The Hidden, werewolves inside didn't get an immediate and physical connection to their future mate. Instead, it was more like a longing, an empty place in their hearts that suddenly felt filled whenever they discovered her. Many of them went outside The Hidden to find their mate while others stumbled upon her before ever discovering the shifter sanctuary. But only a few had ever had their mate come to them while inside their treasured forest.

"If she is, he doesn't deserve her. As soon as we get back, I want to find out why she's out here all by herself."

Blue was right. A lone woman in the Montana mountains didn't make sense. "Agreed. Like I said, Raine. Get going."

Raine grumbled then shifted into his wolf form. His eyes glittered with amber as he twirled in a circle then darted through the underbrush toward the camp.

"So, brother, are we going to keep our word and stay away from her?"

Pete couldn't suppress a smile. He didn't want to, that was for damn sure. But they still had the problem of having no clothes. "Unless you think she'll welcome two butt-ass naked men joining her down there, I think we have to."

* * * *

Blue couldn't help himself. He had to watch her. As he'd done several times already, he eased closer to the pit, careful that she didn't catch him peering down at her. She sat on the ground, her head bowed as she rummaged through her backpack.

He liked her spirit. Most women would've broken down into sniveling crybabies at the sight of three wolves. Then to have one of the wolves jump into the pit with her? Even then she'd held her own. He'd smelled her fear, but she hadn't cowered. Instead, she'd been ready to fight with a pitiful knife as her sole means of protection.

Her dark hair spilled around her shoulders, making his palm itch. It would feel soft against the calluses of his hand, like the smooth belly of a newborn wolf. Although they were hidden now, he remembered the firm swell of her breasts. Her long neck had dragged his gaze from her breasts upward to her pouty lips and her big eyes. Her features had been open, filled more with curiosity than with fear.

"Blue," hissed Pete.

He stepped back, once again heeding his brother's warning to get away from the hole. Dragging in as much of her scent as he could gather, he slunk back to the tree line. "Don't go getting your fur up. She didn't see me."

"Then you're damn lucky. But come on, man. If I can wait to see her again, then so can you. It can't be much longer until Raine gets back. Can't you wait until then?"

Blue relaxed against a tree, hiding the raging need that was tearing up his body. "No problem."

Pete's snort was as soft as his whisper. "Yeah, right. I swear. If you get any hornier, I'm going to have to drag you to the stream and dunk you under."

He was hot for her. There was no denying that. But it was more than that. Maybe it was her bravery, or the glint of challenge in her eyes, or even the underlying impression that she'd had more than her fair share of shit during her lifetime. Whatever it was, he sensed she was special. But just how special?

* * * *

Callie hunkered down against the wall and hugged her knees to her chest. So far she'd managed to keep her fear from taking over, but she was losing ground on that battle fast. She'd clung to the hope of rescue until the moon had finally overtaken the sun. And, although the moonlight was bright, it couldn't reach every part of her prison and she shuddered whenever she heard a sound. The wolves had gone a while ago, but who knew what else might appear?

Did snakes burrow in the ground? If they did, could one come out of the wall and land on top of her? She shook herself and muttered quiet chastisements. She wouldn't let her imagination run wild. If she did, she'd never make it out.

But would anyone ever find her? She'd run into only a few other hikers in the mountains and the prospect of that happening again was minimal at best.

What if she could build a fire? She tugged her backpack closer and dug around until she found a box of matches. But what could she burn? The pit didn't have even a few sticks, much less anything that would make a decent fire. Besides, the possibility of someone seeing the flames from the deep recesses of her confinement was slim. Even if she could get a fire going, she'd have to wait until tomorrow and hope the smoke would draw some attention.

"Damn it all. This sucks."

"Yeah, it kind of does."

Startled, she jumped to her feet and lifted her gaze to find men, drop-dead hunks all three of them, gazing down at her. Two of them had similar facial features and body types. Even the way they held themselves spoke of a common lookout on life. They were relaxed, yet she sensed an underlying energy that could break free at any moment to turn their bodies into quick, sleek machines. One had short hair and wore stubble along his jaw while the other, the one who seemed a little older than his friends, had a shaved head and no facial hair. Even from a distance, she could see their intense blue eyes.

The third, with darker hair and a slighter, albeit still buff-as-possible frame, stood apart from the other two. His dark eyes locked onto hers and, for a moment, she thought of the wolves that had stood over her.

Good grief. Men reminding you of wolves? Don't let your imagination get the best of you. Hang in there.

One of them grinned at her. "But don't get in the dumps. Things can only look up from here, right?" His grin widened. "Or rather, from there."

The one with the shaved head tilted his head at her just as the wolves and Scrunch had done. Once again, she had to tell herself not to compare them to the wolves.

"Knock off the jokes, man." He glanced at the smiling man and back to her. "What are you doing down there?"

Was he serious? Did he think she'd gotten into the pit on purpose? "Oh, you know. Just hanging out." She copied his gesture, leaning her head to the side. "What do you think happened? I fell in and now I can't get out."

The man with the great smile shot her another one. Hell, she swore she could hear him thinking about the commercial where the older woman complained that she'd fallen and couldn't get up. She glared at him, daring him to say so, but he just kept grinning.

"How could you fall? It's not exactly a small hole."

She studied the one with the dark hair. "I was being chased and didn't see it until it was too late. So can you help me get out or what?"

Wait. Do I want them to get me out? Would I be getting out of the frying pan only to land in the flames? Who knows what these guys might do? What are they doing roaming around the woods at night anyway?

But it was either take a chance with them or hope for someone else to come along.

"What was chasing you?" added the grinner.

She noted that he'd asked what and not who. Of course, odds were better that it was an animal instead of a person. "This huge buck charged me. The only thing I could do was to run like hell."

"And he didn't catch you? Bucks are faster than humans."

"I guess fear put a little extra speed into me." What did it matter, anyway?

Mr. Shaved Head went into a crouch, showing off the muscles in his arms as he rested them on his knees. Like his friends, he was dressed casually in jeans and a T-shirt along with worn boots.

They don't carry any packs. That's strange. Unless their campsite is nearby. But at least they aren't carrying any weapons. At least not any I can see.

"I was trying to get far enough ahead that I could climb into a tree when I stopped to grab my bag. I didn't see what was ahead in time and I fell."

"Are you hurt? You didn't seem injured."

She studied the dark-haired man. "No. I'm fine. Physically speaking anyway." Her pride, however, was another thing. But why had it sounded like he already knew the answer? Like he'd seen her before?

"Are you guys going to help me out or what?" On second thought, maybe it was better if she sent them for real help, like a forest ranger or a fireman or a cop. Someone with a uniform and identification so she could know she could trust them. "Maybe you could call the local rescue squad?"

"That would take too long." The one crouching leaned his upper torso so far over the edge that she worried he might tumble in with her.

"No it wouldn't. I can last until tomorrow."

"That's too dangerous."

She suddenly wished he'd grin again. He was right, of course, especially after the creature she'd seen. Although the thing hadn't threatened her, had, in fact, appeared more curious than dangerous. "Then what do you suggest?"

They frowned as one, each of them thrown by her question. She should've begged them to get her out, and instead, she was waiting for them to come up with ideas.

"We'll get you out." Mr. Shaved Head stood up.

She sighed, relieved, and shook off the suspicious thoughts racing through her head. "Okay. So how do we do that?"

"I'll jump down then heft you up to my brothers."

Of course they were related. At least two of them looked like brothers. "Sounds like a plan. Although I'm not thrilled at having you refer to me as something heavy enough to get hefted."

There's that tilt of the head again.

She put everything back into the backpack except for her knife. Trying to do so without them noticing, she slid the knife into the back of her jeans.

"We'll get you out, but you have to promise us something."

Uh-oh. Here it comes.

She tried not to appear miffed, but it was difficult. "You want me to make you a promise?"

What could they want? Recognition as heroes? Money? Or another, more personal type of payment, like submitting to group sex? She didn't consider herself a prude, but she'd never had sex with more than one man and even then she could count the number of times on one hand that she'd gotten intimate.

"Yeah." He cut off Grinner's attempt to protest. "No promise, no help."

Shit and more shit. "Are you really coercing me right now? And you're not going to help me without getting whatever"—she whipped her arms outward in disgust—"you want? Some Boy Scouts you guys are."

He looked surprised and even offended. "It's not like you're thinking. And just so you know, we've never been and never will be Boy Scouts."

She fisted her hands on her hips. "Oh, really? Then tell me. What do I have to do to get you to pull me out of here? What is it you want? Cash? Fame?" She narrowed her eyes. "My *gratitude?*"

They slid their eyes over her body almost at the same time. She felt their lust, but she also felt another element to their perusal. They wanted her. That much was easy to see. But they wanted something else, something even more personal from her. But what could that be?

"There's no reason to get suspicious."

"Then tell me, King, what do I have to promise to do?"

"What the hell does 'King' mean?"

The dark-haired one answered, "I think she's referring to a musical called *The King and I.*"

"Huh?"

"There was this bald king who kept ordering this woman around and—"

He waved off his brother's explanation. "Never mind. You"—he pointed at her—"have to promise you won't run off into the woods."

"I'm not sure what you mean. Run off? Aren't you taking me back down the mountain?"

She gasped when, in one smooth motion, he dropped into the hole. He was impressive, standing well over her five feet, six inches. Close up, his body was even better than before, with muscles rolling into muscles that went on for miles. She'd never liked a shaved-head look on men much, but it only added to his macho appearance. If she hadn't stopped herself, she would've brushed her palm over his head to see how smooth it was. Half to keep from doing that and half out of alarm, she stepped back, plastering her body to the wall.

"Why don't you want me to run off? No one says you have to escort me anywhere."

"We wouldn't want you to get injured trying to get around in the woods at night."

"Which begs the question, what are you three doing out in the woods at night?"

"We can take care of ourselves."

"So can I."

His blue eyes met hers. "Sure you can. After all, you've done so well already."

"You don't have to be such a dick."

"A dick? Is that what you call everyone who comes to your rescue?" Surprisingly, his tone was casual.

"I'm sorry. I shouldn't have called you that. I do appreciate your help." She dragged in a long breath. "It's been a trying day."

"Don't worry about it. Let's get you out of here. Then we can talk on the way back."

"On the way back to where? The city?" *Or your basement where you lock up all the lost women you find?*

His smile, not as brilliant as his brother's, but still warm, lessened her concern. She did what had always served her well. She listened to her gut.

Can I trust him? Can I trust them?

The answer, faster than any other time, came back in a second.

Yes. I can.

But she wasn't good at trusting people. She'd learned the hard way not to let her guard down even when her gut told her she could.

"I'm not going to hurt you." His bluer-than-a-summer-day eyes twinkled. "And trust me. If I wanted to do that, you couldn't stop me."

He was right, but she wasn't about to let him know that. Yet the fact that he'd ignored her question about where they were going didn't help. "Fine. I promise not to take off on my own."

"Good." Then, in another move that was faster than she'd have thought possible, he snatched her pack away from her and hurled it up to the dark-haired man.

"Hey, take it easy with my stuff."

He caught it and slung one strap over his shoulder. "Got it and I didn't hear anything break, either."

"Good to know. Who are you guys anyway? My name's Callie." She didn't give them her last name. If she was wrong about them and she got away, she wouldn't want them to be able to track her down.

He pivoted back to her. "I'm Blue Deacon and those two are my brothers, Raine and Pete."

The one who grinned a lot widened his grin. "Raine here. As you can see, I'm the handsome brother."

"And the modest one, too," added Pete.

"Facts are facts, bro." Raine took the pack from his brother and slipped the straps over his shoulders to rest the pack on his back.

Blue held out his hands, ready to catch her. "Take a jump and I'll heft you out."

"Can you please stop using the word *heft*? It makes me sound like I weigh a ton."

He shook his head. "Shit. From the looks of you, you don't weigh anything at all. Like a feather. Now go."

She took a breath and rushed at him. He caught her easily, then before she had time to worry, he tossed her upward as though she really was as light as a feather. Pete grabbed her arms and pulled her the rest of the way up before setting her on her feet.

She took a moment to get steady and in that time Blue squatted then jumped. He cleared the edge without any help from his brothers and landed on his feet.

"Wow. That was one incredible jump. Are you gymnasts or circus performers?"

Raine laughed. "Hell, no. We're just your everyday, normal kind of guys."

"You are anything but normal." *Oh, hell. I didn't mean to say that.*

Raine shifted the pack into a better position. "I'm not sure if you meant that as a good thing or not."

Embarrassed, she tried to cover. "Um, a good thing. I can take my pack now."

"That's okay. I've got it."

Damn. "You never said where you were taking me."

Blue glanced at his brothers, then turned on his heel toward the trees. "We're taking you home."

Home? Did he mean hers or theirs?

"I'm sorry? Where is home exactly?"

But he didn't answer. Raine waved his hand to gesture her to follow Blue. She paused long enough to find Pete ready to take up the rear, then fell into place, but didn't hurry to catch up to Blue.

It was too bad. She hated to lose her belongings, but it was better that she didn't have the pack to weigh her down. She took in the dark forest around them as they started down a narrow path, reconsidered her options, and decided to take the risk.

Chapter Three

He should've known she'd make a break for it. Raine slung the pack at Pete and started running. It didn't take long before he caught up with her as his brothers had known he would. They hadn't even bothered to give chase, preferring to wait on the path

He let her run, delighting in the way her scent wafted back to him as she pushed through the night air. She'd almost made it to the other side of the clearing before he finally bolted, grabbing her by the legs and bringing her down.

He regretted it the moment he heard her grunt as she hit the ground hard. If he hadn't gotten so caught up in the chase, he would've thought ahead to keep from hurting her. He turned her legs loose to move up her body and she flipped over.

At least he hadn't hurt her so much that she couldn't move.

"Damn it, Callie. I hope I didn't hurt you when I had tackled you. Are you hurt?"

Damn but she smells good.

He couldn't pinpoint the exact aroma. It was a mixture of intoxicating fragrances that tantalized his nostrils. He drew in a long, slow breath, determined to commit her scent to his memory for life.

Her skin glowed under the light of the moon and her chest rose and fell with her uneven, quick breaths. She was even more beautiful than earlier with the rose of excitement coloring her cheeks. Her dark hair spread out around her head, framing her face like a piece of newly discovered art.

He held his body next to hers and felt the press of her firm breasts against his chest. She was lean, athletic, but she still had the rounded body of a real woman. His cock rose to push against her crotch and the heat rising there met with the warmth flowing from between her legs.

Studying the curve of her neck, he let the image of his fangs sinking into the soft flesh rip through him. He'd take her, both her body and her heart, and claim her.

"Callie." Her name was like a song on his lips.

Instead of growing steadier, her breathing quickened. He took another breath and brought in the definite odor of arousal. She wanted him as much as he wanted her. But now was not the time or place to quench either of their needs.

"I hate like hell to say it, but we've got to get back to my brothers. Shit!"

She brought the knife she'd whipped out from behind her to his throat. "Get off me."

"What the hell are you doing? Why are you acting like this? We helped you."

"And I appreciate it. But trying to make me stay with you?" She shook her head. "That's so not happening. I don't like getting ordered around and I'm no one's captive."

He grinned and hoped she'd find it charming. "We weren't ordering you around and you're no captive. Unless we have to make you one to keep you safe."

She pushed on his shoulder and he edged away from her. He rose as she did and gestured toward the knife. "You don't need that, you know."

She held the weapon higher with the sharp blade still pointed at him. "Maybe not, but I'll keep it just the same."

His inner wolf howled in protest, pushing him to jump her and take the weapon away. He could do so before she'd realize what he was doing. He'd push her to her hands and knees, then fuck her from behind. Although he yearned to listen to his wolf, he forced his beast into submission.

"What do you want me to do, Callie? Do you want me to let you roam around the woods alone?"

"I was fine hiking by myself."

"Uh-huh. Yeah, you did a fine job. Which is how you ended up in the bottom of a trap."

She blinked. "What do you mean by calling it a trap? Is it yours? And what were you trying to catch in it? A poor, defenseless female hiker?"

"One, you're not poor or defenseless. And two? It's not mine or my brothers'."

"What's it for?"

He gestured toward the path where his brothers waited. "Blue and Pete are going to wonder what's taking us so long."

"Let them wonder. And answer my question."

"There are these things. They kind of look like wolves, but they're not." He saw her eyes widen and he knew. "You saw one of them, didn't you?"

She recovered, but he'd seen the truth on her face. "I'm not sure. I saw...something."

"Yeah, you saw one, all right. It didn't bite you, did it?"

"No. I was in the hole and it stayed on the outside. What was it? Tell me."

"It doesn't matter now. Just know that they're dangerous. Especially to women."

She was sexy even when she frowned. "Why especially to women?"

They didn't have time to talk about it. Explaining about The Cursed and how they tried to capture human women to mate with would have to wait until she found out about other things first. He didn't like the idea of being without his brothers in the woods either. The Cursed liked to attack at night, and if they got enough of them together, they'd even attack a werewolf. Lately, the attacks had occurred less often, but he wasn't about to push their luck.

"Baby, put down the knife."

"Not a chance. All you have to do is turn around and walk the other way. You guys can keep my camera and all my other stuff."

Had she taken photos of them in their human forms? Or worse, of The Cursed? If she had, then it was a good thing they had the camera in their possession. They couldn't allow pictures of The Hidden and its inhabitants on The Outside, the regular world most people lived in.

"I'm not going without you." He hated acting like a badass, but she wasn't leaving him with any other options. "Either you're going to keep your promise, or I'm going to have to make you keep it."

"Like hell I am. Now get out of here while the getting's good."

Her dark eyes sparkled with alarm, but with courage, too. She was a strong woman, the kind of woman he and his brothers had talked of mating one day. Had fate brought her to them? She'd made it into The Hidden without the aid of another supernatural, which meant she had to be a supernatural being of some kind, too. He sniffed, this time hunting past her alluring smell for any hint of her underlying nature.

She's a werewolf. Or at least part.

He couldn't be sure, but that was the impression he was getting. But, if she was, did she know it? He doubted it. If she did, she would've brought out her fangs and claws to fight him off instead of daring him with a knife.

He'd have to make her come with him. "I wish you'd be more cooperative."

"Fuck you."

She started backing up and he knew she was about to run. He'd catch her easily enough again, but he didn't like the idea of wrestling her for the knife.

"Callie, I'm sorry to have to do this."

He lunged at her, feinting to one side then moving in the other direction and throwing her off guard. Taking her small wrist in his hand, he twisted her arm around to her back and squeezed. She cried out and dropped the knife.

"Let go of me."

"What the hell are you doing?"

Callie and he glanced up in sync to find Blue and Pete standing a few feet away. Although she struggled and she was strong, he took her other wrist and held both arms behind her back.

The corner of Blue's mouth twisted into a snarl. "I asked you what you're doing to her?"

Blue's anger rolled off him in waves that made Raine's hair stand on end. His brother would never hurt him. At least he didn't think he would. Blue was usually the calm and collected one, but that Blue wasn't standing in front of them now.

"She took off. I'm trying to make her see sense."

Pete's eyebrows shot up. "By wrenching her arms behind her back? I'm not sure I like your method of communication, bro."

Did they really think he wanted to hurt her? Did she? Irritation swept over him and he shoved Callie toward his brothers, taking care not to push her hard enough to make her fall. "Here. See if you can make her understand that she can't go off half-cocked in the middle of the night."

She fell into Pete's arms, then pushed away and tried to dart off in a different direction. Pete shouted a curse and grabbed her, pulling her into his arms. She struggled against him, kicking and cursing him as he tried to calm her down.

"See what I said? She won't listen to reason."

Blue's anger had gone, replaced by a sullen recognition of the problem. "Raine, get a couple of those vines over there."

He groaned. "We're tying her up?"

"Unless you have a better idea." Blue's gaze dropped to the knife on the ground. "Or would you rather let her take another stab at you?"

"Nope. I learned that lesson fast enough."

As Pete continued to hold Callie, Raine snatched up the knife, then stalked over to the underbrush and cut off a length of vine. The vine was thin, but it could restrain even a male werewolf. He came back and gave Callie an apologetic look.

"Baby, say you'll come with us. I don't want to have to use this."

At least she'd stopped kicking and stood next to a frustrated-looking Pete who kept one hand locked around her arm. She adopted a sweet smile and tossed her glorious locks. "Sure. No problem. Just turn me loose and I promise I'll come along without a bother."

Raine chuckled then wished he could take it back when she snarled. "You can't expect us to believe you. Please understand that we're doing this for your own good."

"Pff. Yeah, right."

"Will you at least walk between us so I don't have to tie your hands?"

She gave him another sweet, but insincere smile. "Of course I will. I'll do whatever you say."

Blue tore his shirt along the hem then snatched the vine from Raine's hands. "Enough of this. Hold out her hands, Pete."

Pete did as he ordered, putting her hands and wrists together. To Raine's surprise, Callie didn't protest. Not that she didn't want to. He could see her barely controlled anger, but she was smart enough to recognize the futility of fighting them.

"So you're making me your captive."

Raine couldn't deny or confirm her statement. Tying her up was their only option now that she'd refused to cooperate.

Blue wrapped the cloth around her wrists. "This will keep the vine from cutting into your skin." He worked the vine around the padding and tied it, bunching her wrists tightly together.

"It's not too tight, is it, baby?" He hated to see her tied up against her will. Tied up in sexual play would be wonderful, but that was a different thing.

"No." The resistance flowed out of her. "It's okay. I don't blame you. I should've trusted you guys. After all, you did save me."

"And that's all we're still trying to do." Pete rubbed her arms. "Maybe after a bit, we can untie you." He looked to Blue for confirmation.

Blue shrugged, then stalked back toward the path. "Don't make any promises we might not be able to keep."

* * * *

Raine shouldn't like the fact that she'd run, and he didn't. At least not logically. But deep inside him, his wolf paced back and forth, wanting to let her run again so he could chase her. Still, he didn't want her to run, for her sake.

She had to be frightened, of course, but running meant that she hadn't trusted them. Tying her up just made things worse. He watched her, telling himself that he did so because he had to be ready should she try to escape, but that wasn't the real reason. He watched her because he liked doing it.

She was beautiful. But more than that, she was feisty and brave. The fact that she'd been out in the woods alone was evidence of those two attributes. And she was intelligent. He'd seen that the first time he'd looked into her eyes. Granted, falling into the pit wasn't the brightest move, but everyone made mistakes, especially when terrified and attacked by a huge animal.

He'd have to thank Jerry. If Jerry hadn't chased her into the hole, he might never have met her. And not meeting her? Well, that would've been a damned shame.

The movement of her bottom entranced him. She was lean, but the girl still had enough booty for him. The swaying ends of her long hair pointed at her ass, almost as if to say, "Come and put your cock here."

Damn, but how I'd love to do exactly that.

Thinking she was about to stumble, he caught her arm. For a moment, they locked gazes and he kept his hold on her. Then she blinked and tugged her arm away, then started moving forward.

Her legs were long, and even through the material of her jeans, he could tell they were strong. She wasn't a runner, but she had stamina.

How many women could have gotten chased by a wild animal, fallen into a hole, confronted three wolves, then tried to escape? He doubted most could have.

Blue turned back once and caught him studying her ass. His smile came and went, but not before Raine knew that his brother was having the same ideas about her.

That was different. They'd been attracted to other women before, but he'd always known it was only a physical thing. Yet around two years earlier, they'd stopped taking women whenever the need arose. It was almost as if they'd had an agreement that they'd stop before the right woman came along.

Could Callie be that woman?

If they'd met outside The Hidden, he would've known instantly. But, although werewolves in The Hidden didn't get as strong a connection as they might on The Outside, he couldn't ignore the pull he got from her. The question that remained was whether Pete was as entranced by her as he and Blue were.

He spun around, making a complete circle, but that was enough time to see the infatuation on Pete's face. All three of them were thinking the same thing.

Is she the one?

* * * *

Halfway back to camp, Blue relented and allowed Pete to take the binding off her wrists. She'd given it a lot of thought and realized that to go off into the forest when she had no clue where she was would be foolhardy. Instead, she'd have to put her trust in them. The strange thing was that she did trust them. It didn't make sense, but she couldn't help it. They made her feel safe, as though they'd do anything to keep her from harm.

"So how much farther is this camp of yours?" She trudged along, taking care not to trip over anything on the path.

"Not much."

"Way to go, Blue. I wouldn't want to know too much information." She gave Raine a pointed look and brought out another of his wonderful, crooked grins. The men were gorgeous, all buff and tanned. They were three gods come to life in a wilderness fantasy, but they each had different personalities.

Blue was the reserved one. She didn't know if he was the oldest or not, but he seemed to have taken a leadership role over the other two men. He kept his face expressionless for the most part, but when he did smile, it was magical, brightening up his entire demeanor. He was driven, leading the way like a one-track kind of man and rarely joined in the banter between Pete and Raine.

Raine was the jokester. He kept a cheerful expression that was the precursor to his breathtaking grin. Although he kept his voice low at the urging of Blue, he still kept making jokes, sometimes at the expense of his brothers.

Pete was the outsider of the three. He didn't look anything like his brothers, but had adopted mannerisms from both of them. At times, he was as jovial as Raine. Then, without warning, he'd grow serious and become as focused as Blue.

"So you guys are brothers, huh?" She craned around to check Raine's reaction. "I hope you don't mind my saying so, but Pete doesn't have the same family traits that you and Blue have. Let me guess. He's a brother from another mother?"

Instead of getting angry or upset, Raine laughed at her joke. "You might say so. Actually, he's a brother from another mother *and* another father."

She glanced at Pete, who didn't appear to mind them talking about him. "So he's adopted? Sorry, Pete. We shouldn't be talking about you like you're not even here."

"Don't worry about it. I don't have any issues because I'm adopted. If it hadn't been for our parents, I wouldn't have the life I have. And I'm over the problems that came along with my real family."

Raine walked backward a few steps so he could confront his brother, then whirled back around. "What problems?"

"Yeah, right, bro. Just the problem of my mother abandoning me."

"Your mother dumped you? Did you grow up in a foster home?" Did she have that in common with Pete?

"Naw. I went straight from my mom to the Deacons. They're my family now."

"I wish I'd had the same luck. I went through four foster homes before I turned eighteen."

"I'm sorry to hear that."

She disliked getting sympathy, but it didn't bother her coming from Pete.

Pete ignored Raine. "Yep. When the Deacons took me in I gained two awesome parents. It was just too bad that I gained two sorry-ass brothers at the same time."

Raine took a swipe and missed, then whirled around to face forward again. "Ha-ha. You should take that comedy routine on the road."

They lapsed into a comfortable silence and continued on their trek to wherever they were taking her. She decided to try again. "So tell me about this place you're taking me to. Do you have a landline phone? Or a satellite one? Can I use it once we get there? My cell's dead and I couldn't get any reception before anyway. I'd like to call a friend to pick me up."

"We don't have any phones."

Was Blue serious? "None? As in no one in the whole place has a phone? You're kidding."

"Nope. We don't have a lot of things like phones, televisions, or computers. We prefer to live a simple life without all those distractions."

Holy shit, they're taking me to a cult. A backward cult at that. Oh, hell.

Should she try and make another attempt to flee? "How far did you say we had to go?"

"We'll get there when we get there."

She couldn't help but take a jab at Blue. "Wow. That's really deep, man."

"Take it easy, baby."

She whirled on Raine and shoved her finger against his chest. "Don't call me baby. I hate it when men call me baby. Got it?"

"Sure. No problem. No need to poke me." His light attitude put her at ease almost at once.

She blew out a breath and dropped her hands. "I'm sorry. It's a thing with me."

"Then what should I call you? Cute stuff? Or maybe Pussy Cheeks? Hey, how about Snuggle Butt?" He feigned a confused yet hopeful expression. Together the emotions were comical.

She bit the inside of her cheek to keep from laughing. Who could stay angry when he put on such a funny face? "How about you use my actual name?"

Pete leaned on his brother's shoulder. "Naw. That's too formal. We need a term of endearment for you."

"Ours."

She pivoted to find Blue regarding them. "What?"

"We'll call you ours. Because that's what you're going to be. Ours."

At first, she was so flummoxed that she couldn't respond. Was he serious? Or merely joining in the fun? "I'm not yours or anybody else's."

He shrugged then put his back to her. "Maybe not yet, but you will be."

When she opened her mouth to ask Raine what Blue had meant, he shook his head and waved her on. Once again, Pete brought up the rear.

Ours.

What could he have meant other than what she feared he had? Was she being taken captive for them to use as they wished? Although the men were sexy as hell and every inch the wilderness men that filled her wet dreams, she wasn't about to have sex against her will. Would they not only make her their sex slave but give her to other men for fun or profit? Would they make her clean and cook for them, adding insult to the ultimate injury?

She stumbled once and would've fallen if Raine hadn't caught her and kept her upright. As soon as he touched her, her body awakened, betraying her with a yearning that had her breath coming out in quick pants. His mesmerizing gaze met hers, then slid lower to her chest and on to her feet.

"Are you hurt?"

She could've sworn he'd asked an altogether different question. *"Are you hot?"*

"I'm sorry?"

He took his hand away, throwing her off-balance emotionally, and stared at the place where he'd held her. "I asked if you're all right?"

"Oh. Uh, yeah. Are you?" She felt the pink rush of embarrassment in her cheeks. Why had she asked such a stupid question?

He chuckled and swept a strand of her hair out of her face. "Yeah, I'm good." Then, dropping his tone lower, he added, "More than good."

"Keep moving."

At Blue's urging, she put her back to the luscious body of Raine and found her gaze locked on the wide shoulders of Blue. His form didn't bulge like a bodybuilder's, but she could sense he had more strength, more power in his body than two of the barbell junkies ever could. He strode forward, his head moving side to side once in a while, scanning the forest. His graceful movements reminded her of a leopard or mountain lion.

No, nix that. He moves like a wolf. Like fluid, coiled energy ready to be released at a moment's notice.

Her pussy heated up as her nipples pebbled and she had to jerk her attention away. But that didn't keep her mind from going down another road of taboo.

If Raine had wanted to take things further when he'd lain on top of her, would she have let him? Would she have gone along with him? Her pulse quickened as her heart pounded in her chest. Sweat that had nothing to do with their fast trek beaded on her forehead and slickened her palms. She would've spread her legs for him if he'd taken the knife from her then kept her flat on her back. Her blood boiled inside her thinking about how his cock had felt pushed up next to her pussy. She'd inhaled his scent, a strange aroma that made her want him even more. Her tits had rubbed against his chest and an ache had spread through her. An ache that she'd would've voiced if the situation had been different.

She groaned then inhaled and found his scent again, along with his brothers'. Raine and Blue had a similar musky fragrance mixed with sweat and an indefinable wild aroma. Pete had a wild edge to his as well, but his scent was different, spicier than his brothers.

Although Pete was adopted, they acted like brothers. She could see the familiarity between them in the way they communicated, sometimes speaking in fragments while other times all it took was a look. Were they talking about her? Were they as attracted to her as she was to them?

What is wrong with me?

She shouldn't be thinking in those kinds of terms about any of her captors. But she couldn't help it. They hadn't treated her badly other than tying her up. But even now she sensed that they didn't mean her any real harm. They were right. Running off in the middle of the night even in an area she was familiar with was just asking for trouble. But in the woods she didn't know well and in a part of them that she'd never seen before? That was just plain stupid.

They came into a camp almost before she was aware that they'd broken through the underbrush and into a clearing. She stopped, stunned to see tents, huts, cabins, and even a few teepees circling a large area where other people gathered around campfires. The grass was a dark green, greener than she remembered any grass being, while wildflowers of every possible color swayed in a breeze she didn't feel. The scene reminded her of a mix between a Native American tribe and modern-day hippies. The women wore long gowns with moccasin-style shoes while the men wore slacks or jeans, most without a shirt, and a range of footwear from the same shoes the women wore to rough cowboy boots. A few older children dashed around the encampment then stopped to stare at her before returning to their laugh-filled fun.

"Good. You told them we were bringing her back."

Raine nodded at Pete's question. "Isn't it obvious?"

She scanned the area again, but couldn't tell how it was obvious. Pete, however, must've seen the question in her eyes.

"We don't usually wear clothes. Just when we have a newcomer to the group."

Great. They took me to a nudist colony. Well, at least they had enough courtesy to put clothes on for me.

"What is this place?"

"Home."

Pete gestured to those around them. "Stay put and keep to yourself. At least until we say otherwise."

"That sounds ominous."

Raine's grin was forced. "Yeah. It is. A little. Just do as Pete said."

The brothers moved away to greet two men. One was an older man with white hair and a white beard. He held himself in a regal stance even though he leaned on a cane as he listened to Blue. The other was tiny, barely standing over three feet, and yet he didn't have the characteristics of a little person. Instead, he reminded her of the elves in her favorite childhood books with his red hair, fair skin, and large feet.

"What the hell am I going to do? I've been abducted and forced deep into the woods. Not at all what I'd planned on when I started this trip," she muttered.

Blue glanced back as though he'd heard her even though she was sure she'd spoken too softly. Did he have sensitive hearing like her?

She darted her gaze away from his and studied the people around her. They were of different ethnicities, sizes, and ages, but they all appeared to have one thing in common. Their faces were filled with joy.

What the heck is going on here? How can everyone be so damn happy? Unless they're all drinking the Kool-Aid.

Was everything as idyllic as it seemed? Or were they brainwashed to the bone?

"That's not possible."

She jerked back to see the older man glaring at her. The protest that she hadn't chosen to come was on her lips, but Pete shot her a warning look. Deciding that it was safer to follow their rules for now, she pressed her lips together and tried to act like fear wasn't taking a hard hold on her.

"Yes, but I'm only telling you what I know. She wasn't anywhere near the water, Charlton." Blue stood straight and tall, but she could see an underlying uneasiness in the way he shifted back and forth on his feet. The fact that the white-haired man called Charlton made him nervous was apparent.

"But it was The Time of Coming," added Raine. "That much we know. And remember what Jerry said about the odd sensation he felt when he chased her? Could another portal be open? One in the forest?"

Who's Jerry? I didn't see a man there.

Charlton kept quiet as his smaller friend shook his head vigorously. "Anything is possible in The Hidden. But let's hope not. Still, even if that's true, she shouldn't have been able to enter on her own."

"And yet she did. Jerry wasn't touching her when she came through. She led him inside then fell into the pit The Cursed dug. She's lucky they abandoned the trap a while ago."

Came through what? And what is a Cursed?

"Which, again, isn't possible." Raine rubbed the back of his neck.

"Unless she's one of us." Pete brought her closer to Charlton, then gave her a quick, comforting smile before shifting his attention back to the group.

"That, at least, would make sense." Charlton studied Blue, his own eyes a deeper shade than Blue's. "Do you feel anything about her?"

What is he supposed to feel? Damn it all, why don't they let me in on their discussion?

She had to refrain from demanding answers. If she did, she knew one of the men would end up hauling her away. She might never get any answers if she made them angry.

Charlton leaned on his cane, but she got the impression that he didn't really need the crutch. His body was fit and possessed a strength not shown in brawn. "Let's not discuss this anymore outside. I'll call the other members of The Council and we'll come to a decision. Meet us in the cabin once you have her settled in your tent."

"Our tent?"

"Yes, Blue. Yours. Who else's home should she stay in?" The stern expression on Charlton's face softened. He patted Blue on the shoulder. "I doubt you'll find her too much of a hardship."

"Fine. If that's what you think is best."

Pete edged closer to Charlton and said something she couldn't hear. Charlton's hard look returned and his piercing blue eyes landed on her again. He gave Pete a curt nod then spun around and strode away. The small man started to speak then clamped his mouth closed and twirled around to scurry after Charlton.

Blue took one look at her, nodded at Pete who took the backpack from Raine, then motioned for Raine to follow him as he walked in a different direction—away from her.

Pete stood for a moment then waved her over to him. She tried not to hurry, but she did feel more comfortable closer to him. Yet halfway there, she slammed to a stop and gaped at the animal at the edge of the tree line. The buck that had chased her dropped his head then shook his mighty antlers before springing back into the forest.

"That's him! That's the buck that chased me." She pointed, uncaring if she made a scene and drew everyone's attention. "Did you see him?"

Pete took her arm and pulled her along with him, slinging her pack over his shoulder. "Yeah, I saw him. That's Jerry."

"Jerry? He has a name?" She craned her neck back trying to find him and almost fell. Pete kept her on her feet as he pushed through the opening of a large tent, bringing her along with him.

The tent was huge and unlike any tent she'd ever seen except in the movies. Gloriously colored quilts lay everywhere while candles rested on wooden platforms. A hole in the top of the tent let out the smoke that would come from the fire pit directly below it. It was like a sheik's tent and all that was needed was the beautiful harem women.

Is that what I'm supposed to be?

"Jerry isn't a pet. He's our friend."

"O-kay." Lots of people considered their pets their friends and even part of the family, but a buck? "But your friend chased me into a hole."

"He didn't mean to." Pete released her arm then dropped her backpack.

"Oh, well, then, that's good to know. Listen, I don't know what this place is, but I know it's not where I want to be."

"I wish it was."

Had she heard him right? "What did you say?"

Pete ducked his head then brought it back to give her the most incredible look she'd ever had. The heat in his eyes could've melted her on the spot and her pussy clenched as that heat shot out of him and into her. He was smoldering inside for her and had ignited a flame in her. The need, however, was tinged with another element, one born of the yearning she'd sensed earlier. He wanted her body, but he wanted more than that.

"What did your brother mean? Why did he say I'm yours?" Did she really want to know?

"He meant what he said." He tilted his head at her. "He wants you as much as I do."

She didn't step back when he took a step toward her. Still, she had to leave, had to get away before she lost her will to get back down the mountain. He grabbed her roughly and it took her a few moments before she tried to tug out of his hold.

"No. I don't want this." She pushed away from him, but he held on. She stared at him, then whimpered and pulled back. But not hard enough to break free. "Let me go." Her voice came out weak and shaky as though she hadn't meant what she'd said. Had she? She yanked again.

He suddenly let go, sending her falling to the floor. Her landing was softened by the quilts made of a material she'd never seen.

"Yes, you do." He fell to her side and bent over her. He gripped her behind the neck and lifted her head. He brushed his mouth close to hers, lightly, teasing her. And damn it if his tease didn't work.

She reached up and took him by the hair to crush his lips against hers. At first he let her take the lead, but it wasn't long before his grip tightened on her. He pulled her lower lip between his teeth as she tried to do the same to his upper lip.

She moaned, not caring if anyone outside could hear. She hadn't realized it earlier, but she'd wanted this to happen. Almost from the first moment she'd seen the Deacon brothers, she'd wanted them. Not just Pete, but his brothers, too. Did the knowledge that Blue wanted her, too, upset him? She shoved away the question of what he'd think.

He deepened the kiss, making it harder yet softer at the same time. Nibbling on her lower lip gave way to giving her his tongue and she took it with relish. She sucked on it, drinking in every drop of his taste, then offered him hers in return.

He groaned and cupped her breast to rake his thumb over her nipple. She arched, urging him to do anything he wanted. The rumble of a growl rolling through his chest didn't scare her. In fact, it had the opposite effect. Excitement rushed into her and, if he hadn't had his mouth on hers, she would've asked him to make the sound again.

When he ended the kiss, she was left trying to breathe, trying to think straight, but it was as impossible for her to do as flying to the moon. "How do you do that?"

Hunger flashed in his eyes. "How do I do what?"

She fisted her hands on her hips. "You know damn well what I mean. How do you make me—"

He pressed his mouth against hers, cutting off her question. The kiss was different than the first, more leisurely, more sensual, more seductive than any kiss she'd ever experienced. He took her lips, at first tender, then tempting her to take the kiss further. He traced a path along them with his tongue as though asking permission to enter a second time. She gave it and moaned, enjoying the intoxicating taste she'd already started missing.

Snaking his arms around her waist, he pulled her torso closer, flattening her breasts against his solid chest. She inhaled the spicy scent that tingled the insides of her nostrils and had her breathing in fast for more of it. Sliding her arms over his wide shoulders, she let her fingers explore the muscles that strained against the material of his shirt. She locked her fingers behind his neck and held on.

He slipped a hand lower and cupped her butt cheek. Her heart sped up along with the throbbing of her pussy.

She wished she'd worn a skirt. Anything except her usual jeans. Heat boiled inside her and she bent one knee, spreading her legs in invitation. He accepted and moved his hand around to find the button of her jeans. She clutched him tighter and shifted her body to make it easier for him.

Callie recognized his power as she'd recognized his brothers'. Their bodies were hard, but they had an inner strength that she didn't quite understand. It was that strength that drew her to them like a moth to a flame and she didn't care if she'd crash and burn against their light. At that moment, she would've risked anything and everything to have him.

When he'd gotten her zipper down, she lifted her hips and let him slide her jeans and panties down her legs. He stopped kissing her long enough to mumble a curse as he yanked her boots off so he could rid her of her clothes. He paused, taking in her body, then slid his fingers along her leg.

"I need you so much."

She should've insisted that they stop. She should've grabbed her clothes and dashed away. But it was too late. It had been too late from the moment she'd seen him and his brothers.

Can I have Raine and Blue, too?

The exhilarating idea gave her the courage to go on. She'd always been so careful, so responsible in anything to do with sex, but now he'd turned loose a part of her that she hadn't even realized was caged. She smiled as she pictured a wild animal breaking free inside her. The image of a wolf with fur the color of her hair slashed through her mind and her smile grew wider.

If only that were real.

But that was ridiculous. How could that ever be? And yet, somewhere deep inside her, she thought she heard a howl.

She arched against him, urging him to take her. Cupping his bulging crotch, she closed her eyes and fumbled with his button. If she didn't get his cock out soon, she'd explode with need.

She hadn't made much progress in getting his jeans undone when he surprised her by dropping her back on the quilts. She opened her eyes to find him standing over her, hurriedly stripping his jeans off. He wore no underwear, and as soon as it was free of its constraints, his cock shot out, hard, long, and oozing pre-cum.

She swallowed and wondered if he was too big. Could she handle a man his size? Whether she could or not, she'd damn well do her best and try. She sat up and pulled off her top along with the sports bra she wore.

He inhaled, his focus intent on her breasts, and for the first time in her life, she worried that she wasn't big enough or perky enough. But those fears soon left her as she took in his desire, his gaze skimming down her body, then up again to linger on her breasts before moving to her face.

"You're incredible."

Had he sensed her worry?

"Every damn inch of you is incredible."

He tugged off his shirt and fell on top of her. His hands skimmed over her, along her legs, slipping to her inner thighs, then teasing her as he touched her pussy then moved over her stomach to take a breast. Bits of amber flashed in his eyes.

He pressed his mouth to hers again as she clenched his back. She concentrated on the hard, hot flesh searing her palms as she skimmed her hands over all the ridges and valleys of his body.

Pete gripped her harder, rubbing her clit and sinking his finger into her pussy until she wanted to scream at him to fuck her. Only his mouth on hers again stopped her cries. He lashed his tongue with hers, daring her to try and keep it in her mouth.

She was about to make good on her scream when he pulled back. He studied her, his finger still in her pussy, yet unmoving.

"Do you want me?" His voice was low to the point of changing his words into a growl.

"What?" she whispered. "Can't you tell I do?"

She'd expected a chuckle, but he was too serious. His hand picked up a steady rhythm that nearly drove her insane. Her abdomen tightened. She tried to bring his mouth back to hers, but he shook free of her hold.

"What are you doing?" Her breathing was ragged, showing how

much she was on the edge and needing him.

"I want to look at you. I want to remember the first time we're together."

A groan broke free and she hit him on the shoulder. A girl could only stand so much. "You can look at me later. Hell, stare at me all night if you want. But right now, I need you to fuck me."

He flicked his tongue over her nipple all while keeping his eyes locked to hers. "What about foreplay?"

"Screw foreplay." She grinned. "No. Better yet. Screw me."

He chuckled, the rich sound flowing over her. "Yes, ma'am."

She stared in horror at him and struck him again. "Don't ever call me that again. You got that?"

"Don't worry. I hated it the minute it left my mouth."

She laughed, happy that he'd had the same thought. "So? Are you going to do it, or are you going to take a picture? It'll last a lifetime."

"I want more than a damn picture for the rest of my life."

She frowned, once again thrown. "The rest of your life? Ours? What are you two saying?" Her heart pounded. Had she known him longer, his words would've captured her heart. But it was too early, too unexpected for that kind of talk. As far as she planned, she'd probably never see him or his brothers after tomorrow.

Without warning, pain seared into her, putting a tight ring around her heart. She didn't want to think about never seeing them again. But why? She didn't know them. Denying the raging lust inside her, she shoved him back and fisted her hands on his chest. "We need to stop. I don't understand—"

"You will. In time. Until then, don't think."

"But—"

"Callie?"

She waited for him to go on. "Uh-huh?"

"Don't take this the wrong way, but would you please shut up? Do you want me to fuck you or not?"

She started to open her mouth again then bit her lower lip and nodded instead. He pushed her on her back and shoved her legs apart with his. Gazing into her eyes, he thrust his cock into her.

She cried out, a quick, sharp pain coming along with his size, but her cry changed into moans as he worked his hips back and forth. Her pussy walls enclosed him, welcoming him as she enveloped him in her arms.

He kissed her neck, nibbling her flesh as he pumped into her with a steady, strong rhythm. Wrapping her legs around him, she pushed back, giving him as much as he gave her. His balls spanked her bottom, and vaguely, she wondered if he'd like to use his hand against her butt cheeks instead. But that would have to wait for another time.

Another time.

She sighed. Would there be another time? If not, then she wanted to remember tonight as much as she could.

He placed his forehead against her shoulder and his short pants echoed in her ear. She stroked his neck, letting his hair tickle the side of her hand.

The heat that she'd thought was as hot as it could go leapt higher still. Her abdomen stirred with passion as her climax neared. And when he reached down to stroke her clit, she couldn't hold back any longer.

Her orgasm burst free, shooting waves of lust through her body in tremendous waves. She shook, her eyes closed, and rode the ride as it sped up then shuddered into the end.

Pete lifted away from her, and without looking, she knew he watched her face. He rammed into her harder, faster than before. Then, just as she opened her eyes, she saw his face tense along with his body. He stayed on the precipice for a few moments, the determination in his face showing how much he wanted to last longer, then yelled as he thrust into her again. His body shook as his release tore out of him and into her.

When at last he was finished, he fell to her side with his arm slung over her stomach in a protective way that had her tearing up.

Only then did she stop to think about real protection.

Oh, shit.

"Uh, Pete?"

"Yeah, sweetie."

She turned to stare at him. "That is so not any better than calling me baby."

"Sorry. Yeah, Callie?"

"I know this is a little late and it's kind of like we should've watched a Lifetime movie beforehand, but I'm..."

He swept his palm over her cheek and she found herself leaning into the caress. "You're...what?"

"I'm not on anything."

"On any what? Drugs?" He chuckled. "That's good to know. But I'd stick by you through rehab."

She slapped his arm. "Funny. No, that's not what I mean. I'm not on birth control."

"Oh, that." He flopped onto his body, seemingly undisturbed by her revelation.

He'd thrown her with what he'd said, but did his eyes have less amber in them? "Oh, that? Because unless you snuck on a condom, we might regret what we did."

He rolled back onto his side. "I could never regret making love with you."

Wow. Did he just say that?

"Besides, Callie, it's not a problem."

"Huh? What does that mean?" Was he sterile? Or snipped?

"Hey, Pete."

She gasped and grabbed for her clothes at the sound of the voice outside the tent. Pete signaled that it was nothing to worry about.

"Yeah, Luke?"

"They want to see you in there."

To her surprise, he jumped to his feet and pulled on his jeans. He didn't bother picking up his shirt. "I'm coming."

"Hey, hang on. We have things to talk about."

"It'll have to wait."

She clutched her clothes over her body and sat up. "But you guys are going to take me down the mountain tomorrow, right?"

The expression on his face didn't give her reassurance.

"I'm sorry, Callie, but that will depend on what Charlton and the rest of The Council decide. Until then, you have to stay here." He motioned around him. "Feel free to make yourself at home. My brothers and I will return as soon as we can, but that may not be until the morning."

"Wait. You're leaving me? Alone?"

"Not really. Someone will stand guard over you." He hurried to add the rest. "To protect you, of course."

"To protect me from what?" *Or is it to keep me from running?*

But he was gone before she could get an answer.

Chapter Four

Callie pushed through the flaps of the tent. Pete was nowhere to be seen, but then it was difficult to see past the very large man standing in her way.

"Excuse me, but did you see where Pete went?" She hoped the man knew who Pete was.

"Yup."

Okay, he's not much of a talker.

She put on her sweetest smile. Why did he remind her of a stuffed teddy bear? "Do you know where he went?"

"Yup."

Oh. My. God. Really. Is he a one-word man?

But she didn't let her exasperation show. Maybe she needed to get more personal with the big lug. "You wouldn't happen to be Luke, would you?"

"Yup."

She nodded, thinking that it might encourage him to elaborate. But that tactic failed. "Great. Um, you're a big, strong guy, huh?"

"Guess so."

"I bet you have lots of women throwing themselves at you."

He didn't answer, letting his perplexed expression do his talking.

So much for getting more chummy with him. "Do you think you could take me to him? Or to Blue or Raine?"

"Nope."

She blinked, maybe because she'd just noticed that he hadn't blinked at all. "Why not?"

"Can't."

*I've never wanted to shake an answer out of anyone more than I
do right now.*

"Why can't you?"

"Just can't."

The last thread of her patience broke. "Look, big guy. If you can't,
then how about you pointing me in the right direction and I'll find
them myself?"

"I'm yours."

His large, flat face scrunched up in what she thought might be a
pout. "I'm sorry? How are you mine?" Did every man she met in the
woods want her?

"I'm the one Blue picked to watch you."

"Oh, he did, did he?" But what did that mean? Again she had to
wonder if Blue had gotten him to watch her to keep her safe? Or to
watch her to keep her from leaving?

"Tell you what, Luke. I'm going to have a look around the camp."
She held up her hand in what she thought was the Girl Scout salute. "I
promise I won't go into the woods. Is that good?"

He nodded vigorously, shaking the mane of dark hair to spill
around his face. His bare chest was even broader than Blue's and
covered with hair. He was a bear of a man in more than his size. "Stay
in the camp. The woods can be bad at night."

She didn't bother asking how the woods could be bad since she
had other matters to attend to. First, she'd find the men and then she'd
extract a promise from them to take her down the mountain in the
morning. Or at least put her in a place where she could find her own
way home.

"Great. Then that's settled." She started past him when he thrust
out a huge paw of a hand.

"Nope. Stay put."

She fought back the urge to make a break for it. He was huge, but
she'd seen big men who were fast. She had to find another tactic to
use. "I thought you said I could walk around?"

"Nope. Changed my mind."

She resisted the urge to ask him how big a mind he had. "I just want to see if I can scrounge up a little food. Is that so bad?"

His unibrow lifted skyward. "You're hungry? Sure, sure." Craning his tree-trunk-size neck around, he hollered, "Lyra, bring food!"

Crap. That didn't work either.

Within a few seconds, a beautiful woman with flowing brown hair appeared out of the darkness carrying a basket. She was as tall as Luke with what would be considered a large frame for a woman, but the way she held her body, the way her emerald eyes sparkled, gave her a special appearance that was entrancing.

"I was already on my way." She jutted out her chin. "And don't you go yelling for me like I'm your slave, Luke Yahr. I may be your mate, but I'm not about to take orders from you."

She ignored the fact that Luke tried to respond and shifted her attention to Callie. "I'm Lyra."

"And I'm Callie."

"I heard we had a visitor and expected that the Deacon brothers hadn't bothered to think about food. What else would you expect from men?"

Callie liked her. Her warmth was genuine and her demeanor easy-going. "I guess. I don't really know them since I just met them earlier."

Lyra pushed her way into the tent and Callie followed behind her. She set the basket down on the bright blue quilt in the center of the tent nearest the fire pit then turned back with a smile on her face and a twinkle of curiosity in her eyes. "Really? Are you sure about that?"

Callie fought to keep from darting her gaze to the quilts where she and Pete had made love. Would Lyra be able to tell by how rumpled the blankets were? Or worse, to smell the lingering scent of their sex? "I'm not sure what you mean."

That's it, isn't it? Like he'd said. It had felt more like making love than having sex. Like I've known him for a lot longer than a few hours.

Lyra gave her a secretive smile. "Would you like to eat alone? Or would you prefer to have company?"

Since she wasn't going to get away from the tent, she might as well get as much information from Lyra as she could. "Please, join me."

Callie settled on the quilt opposite from where Lyra sat and waited for her to open the basket. The tall woman pulled open the lid and started putting out a variety of foods, all of which were either vegetables or fruits. "The men should have a container of water around here. Ah, there it is."

She reached over and grabbed a pitcher and two mugs off a low-lying shelf then poured them both a drink. "I'm sorry, but I didn't have any meat to serve you."

"So you're not vegetarians?"

Lyra's laugh sounded like a cackle, but it didn't take away from her charm. "Some of us are. Not Luke or myself, though. Or the Deacon brothers. Tell me. What did you think of them?"

She hadn't expected that question. "Like I said, I just met them."

Lyra rubbed an apple on the skirt of her dress. "As soon as I saw Luke I knew he was the one for me. And he knew it, too. Although I think it took me a while to actually admit it. But that's the way of it, isn't it? Something wonderful comes in such a quick time that the logical side of you thinks it's too good to be true."

"I'm not sure I understand what you mean. Are you talking about love at first sight?" Surely, Lyra didn't think she'd fallen for the Deacons.

"For me and Luke, it was. But for others?" She shrugged. "Who knows? I wouldn't doubt that those men had their fair share of women who would've lain with them the first night of knowing them."

Callie dropped her gaze to pick up a banana. Was Lyra hinting that she knew about her and Pete?

"They're terrific men, you know. Better than most, I'd say. The woman who gets them as mates will be a very lucky girl."

"You said that word before. Mate. Do you mean like a husband and wife? Or partners?" She peeled the banana then it hit her. "Did you mean one woman for all three of them?"

Lyra bit into her apple and took her time chewing the piece. "So how did you meet them?"

Way to avoid answering.

But Callie didn't think she should push. "I almost hate to tell you."

Interest brightened Lyra's face. "Well, then, now you have to. It sounds like a good story."

"Yes, I guess it is. Although it makes me feel a bit stupid for how it happened." She took a bite before going on and took the time to chew and think about her answer. "I was hiking through the woods."

"On The Outside."

"I'm not sure what you mean."

Lyra waved her confusion away. "Never mind. Go on."

"Anyway, I saw this amazing buck with great antlers and I started to take his picture." Did Lyra's enthusiasm suddenly wane?

"But when I did, he saw me and charged. I was so stunned I barely thought to grab my camera. Once I did, I took off running and ran straight into a big hole."

"No! Was it a deep hole? Like a pit or a trap?"

"Yeah. How'd you know?"

"I've seen them before. So is that when they found you?" Lyra leaned forward, anticipating the rest of the story.

"No. It was strange, but first there was this animal who watched me. I'm not sure what it was."

Lyra's face darkened. "Did it have red eyes?"

"Yes, it did. Do you know what I'm talking about? Have you seen it?" Eagerness zipped through her.

"I have and you were lucky that it didn't do anything other than watch you."

The venomous tone of Lyra's voice had her rearing back. "It didn't seem all that vicious to me. What is it? I've never seen anything like it."

"Is that when the Deacon men showed up? Did they run it off?"

It seemed Lyra was an expert at avoiding questions. But again, she decided not to push. "No. You'd think I'd sent out invitations. After the creature left, then three wolves showed up. That's when I really got afraid."

"Really? Did they act like they'd hurt you?"

She stopped to recall how they'd paced around the hole. Yet they really hadn't done anything threatening. Even when the dark wolf had jumped into the hole, he hadn't attacked. "No. Now that you bring it up, they didn't. One even got within a foot of me and didn't bite. I guess I was lucky."

"You're luckier than you know." Lyra leaned back and rested her weight on her elbows. "Then what happened?"

"The wolves left, and after a while, that's when the Deacon brothers showed up."

"What a wonderful story."

"You're being nice. I look like an idiot. Hell, I am an idiot for running straight into a hole."

Lyra finished her apple in a couple of bites that any longshoreman would've been proud of. "What else were you supposed to do? Let the buck run over you?"

"Thanks for saying that." She took another bite of her banana then followed it with a long drink. "So what is this place, anyway?"

Lyra's face lit up with joy. "It's our home. I suppose others might think of us as a cult or some kind of commune, but it's not that. We call our home The Hidden since we're so protected from outside interference by the mountains. We like to live in a simple way without all the modern conveniences."

She laughed at Callie's shocked expression. "I can understand your reaction. At first you think, what will I do without a washing machine? Or a hot bath to soak in? But, trust me, this place has so much more to offer. I bet once you get to know us, you won't ever want to leave."

The remainder of her banana dropped to the quilt. "Wait a minute. You make it sound like I'm staying. I'm leaving in the morning. No matter what." She'd added the last part as a challenge.

Lyra pulled back, her mouth parting in an *oh*. "I'm sorry. I didn't mean to upset you. Maybe I should go. The Deacon men should explain all this to you. Not me."

She stood, not bothering to gather any of the food, and scurried to the exit. "Please enjoy the food."

"No, Lyra. Stay. I have a lot more questions." She jumped up after her and made it outside to see Lyra dashing away. Luke put his brawny frame in front of her, blocking her from leaving again. She scowled at him but didn't try to get around him. What was the point? She'd never make it.

What the hell is going on?

* * * *

Blue stood next to his brothers and faced the members of The Council. Charlton sat at the low long table along with Xnax, the firemaker, Tina, a fairie, Wisa, a werecat, and Harrison, a werewolf that he and his brothers didn't like very well. The newest member, Titto, one of the few elves in The Hidden, propped his feet on top of the table.

"As we were saying, we believe another opening has formed. Jerry said he felt it, too. We'll send a few people back to the pit and see if they can locate it during the next Time of Leaving. If it's true that it exists, we'll need to come up with precautions to watch over it." Charlton stroked his beard as he spoke, his blue eyes sliding from Blue, to Raine, and then to Pete.

Blue took a deep breath and confirmed what he thought he'd

smelled as soon as Pete had walked into the cabin. He glanced at his brother, who in the same instant found the floor very interesting.

He had her.

Turmoil roared to life in his gut. On one hand, he wished Pete had waited, giving them time to explain where she was and how they might not be able to take her back down the mountain. On the other hand, he couldn't blame him. If he'd had time alone with her he might've done the same thing. The whole time they'd walked to camp, he'd felt her allure and had fought against acting on his impulse to shove her to the ground and take her. She'd held a hold over him, one that he couldn't explain. Not unless he considered the possibility that she was their intended mate.

If they were lucky, The Council wouldn't pick up the scent of sex from Pete. That might make things even more complicated than they already were.

Could she be the one? If they'd met her on The Outside, they would've instantly known. The connection all werewolves felt for their mate would've taken hold of them and left no doubt. But it was different within The Hidden. The instant bond wasn't felt the same way. Of course the attraction was there, but it was a different sensation, more a feeling that an emptiness had been filled. Yet wasn't that how he'd felt when he'd seen her? Was he ready to admit that he'd sensed that special something about her? He wished he'd taken the time to talk to his brothers about it. If only he had experienced it, then it was nothing. But if all three of them had? Then that was definitely a sign none of them could ignore. He needed more time to find out.

"There's still the question of how she was able to come inside without the help of one of us." Titto's red hair matched the ball of fire dancing in Xnax's hand.

"Obviously, she has to be a supernatural. Or at least have it in her blood. Otherwise, she'd have never made it in."

"Xnax is right. But if she's not, then what happens when someone who isn't one of us runs into this strange, invisible barrier? Will they get through, too? Will they even feel it? Will they touch it? Or will it keep them from getting near? A portal like this could be devastating."

Everyone grew quiet and considered Raine's questions. They couldn't have humans running into the barrier then shouting about it to others on The Outside.

"That's why we'll have to watch over it." Charlton twisted toward Harrison. "You have family near here. One who knows of The Hidden? Isn't that right?"

Harrison jerked as though coming out of a trance. "Uh, yes. I could ask one of them to try and get through. Of course, I'll have to wait for the next Time of Coming. But I wouldn't mind spending a little time on The Outside."

"Good. That part of our discussion is settled. We'll send a party to check on the new portal and Harrison's human family member will try and make it through." Charlton rested his elbows on the table, but Blue could see that he wasn't finished, but waiting for another matter to be broached.

"Another question is which kind of supernatural is she?" Tina's silver eyes landed on Pete then narrowed.

"Does that matter?" Blue kept his voice level, not wanting to challenge the fairy.

Although often perceived in literature as fun, caring, and sweet creatures, many fairies could be a pain in the butt and a tough enemy. Right now it was her sense of smell that was almost as good as a werewolf's that worried him. If she picked up on Pete's after-sex aroma, she wouldn't hesitate to mention it.

Blue checked Harrison to see if he'd picked up the sexual fragrance, too. But Harrison was often oblivious to the world around him, choosing instead to focus on wine and making love to his mate, Edwina. How he'd gotten on The Council was a mystery to Blue.

"And does she know what she is? From the way you describe your interactions with her, I don't think she does." Wisa, her elongated face a reminder of her cat inside, lifted her head and sniffed.

Crap.

"I don't think she knows about supernaturals in general, much less that she has that kind of blood in her."

Tina's mouth widened in a small, but very cheerful grin. "Do you smell what I smell?"

Blue's stomach dropped to the floor. He risked a glimpse at Pete and saw the answer written all over his face. Pete was an open book and couldn't hide his emotions.

"Do you feel a connection with her, Pete?"

Pete cleared his throat and met Charlton's gaze. "Yes." He cleared his throat. "I don't know."

"But you've already slept with her?"

Again, Pete could no more lie than a skunk could change its stench. "Yes." He held his head higher. "You know I've stayed away from the females here and on The Outside for the past couple of years. Now I know why."

Charlton arched an eyebrow and pursed his lips. "I was going to recommend that you take the woman down the mountain tomorrow before dawn arrived so she wouldn't see any more than she already has. But now I'm not sure."

"Let's remember that they didn't bring her here." Titto slapped his hands down on the table, rattling the cups set before the members. "They didn't seek her out."

"So? We've had others who have come inside and found their mates."

Thanks, Xnax. He shot the fire maker a grateful look.

"As long as she turns out to be their mate, then no harm is done. But do we let them take the time to find out?" Xnax tossed his ball of fire into air and caught it with his other hand. "Or would it be safer to kick her out now?"

Forget that. Thanks for nothing.

"Give us the time."

All eyes turned to Pete. Raine jumped in to add his support. "Yes. Give us the time."

"Is that what you want to do, Blue?"

Blue couldn't have let his brothers stand on their own if he'd wanted to. And he didn't want to. "Yes."

"And if it turns out you're just hot for her and she's not really your mate? What do we do? She'll know too much by then." Tina dropped her chin and studied them one at a time.

"I don't know." He had to be honest.

"Another could claim her." Xnax had yet to look at any of them.

He was right. When supernaturals lost their mate, they had the right to claim another, especially if the woman's intended mates couldn't or wouldn't claim her. The thought of another man or men having Callie in their bed made Blue's stomach churn. "That won't happen. I'm standing here now and taking responsibility for her."

"As do I," added Pete. Raine nodded his agreement. Although they'd each jumped on board with Blue's decision, he could tell that they were still nervous about it. They'd known her for less than a day and had barely spent any time with her. On The Outside, where the connection was often instant, that wouldn't be a problem. But in The Hidden? Getting to know the intended mate was sometimes necessary first.

But what else can I do? Leave her to fend for herself? Yeah, right. That's the reason I said I'd stand up for her.

Charlton glanced at the members to his right, then to his left. Each gave their consent with their silence. "Very well. But don't let things get out of hand."

How would he handle it if she wasn't the one for them? Could he let her leave with knowledge about their home? Would The Council ever allow it? Or would he have to keep her with them, thus keeping their community's tightly guarded secret? Blue tried to appear confident as he motioned for his brothers to leave before him, but he was anything but that.

Raine was the first to question him once they were far enough away not to be heard. "Did we just do what I think we did?"

"If you mean putting ourselves on the line for her, then yeah. We did." Even if he'd messed up by doing so, Blue wasn't about to go back on his word. And he didn't think he'd messed up.

"I'm okay with it." Pete surged ahead of them, a clear sign that he had more to spill but wanted them to coax it out of him.

Blue exchanged glances with Raine and hurried to Pete's side. "You're saying that because you've already taken her to your bed. Our bed."

"He's right, isn't he? In the short time we left her with you, you got between her legs."

Pete kept up a brisk pace, neither denying nor confirming Raine's assessment. He'd almost reached their tent when Raine took his arm and spun him around to face him. "So what do you think? Is she the one?"

The small smile on Pete's face said as much. "Yeah. She is. Didn't Blue already say as much when we were bringing her back? Hell, he told her as much. He called her ours. My actions only confirmed it. She's our intended mate."

"I may have jumped the gun on telling her that."

Pete gaped at him. "You're not serious. How can you doubt it? Why else would you have taken responsibility for her?"

Raine's perusal made him nervous. His brother had always been able to see through him. "Maybe. But I think we need to take this at a slower pace. Just to be certain."

"What the hell for? Pete's already had her and I want my time alone with her. She makes me feel…whole. Isn't that what it's all about? Isn't that what our mate is supposed to make us feel?"

"Yeah, bro. What more proof do you need?" Pete clamped a hand on Raine's shoulder. "He's right. She makes me feel the same way. Before and after I took her."

They were right. He'd experienced the same odd but wonderful sensation. "I want to be sure it's not a matter of our lack of female company for the past two years."

Pete growled out his words. "This isn't a case of being horny, man."

"He's right. Besides, we all agreed that our lack of libido during that time was a result of our getting ready for her. Like The Universe telling us that she was coming."

"Yeah. Two years is a long time to go without the sacrifice meaning something."

"If that's the case, then where's the rush? We've waited this long for her. We can wait a little longer." He focused his gaze on Pete. "Or at least Raine and I can."

"Speak for yourself, man."

Blue grabbed his younger brother behind the neck. "Okay, hot dog, let's agree to leave her alone for tonight at least. She's probably tired, anyway."

Pete's grin blasted onto his face. "You can count on that. I think I wore the girl out." He almost didn't move fast enough to dodge Raine's punch. "Hey, hate the game, man. Not the player."

Blue crossed his arms and watched as his brothers roughhoused their way closer to their tent. But they weren't fooling him. "This way, guys. Let's get a run in tonight." If anything could distract them from Callie, it'd be a long run through the woods.

Tearing off his shoes and clothes, he let the wolf inside him roar to life. The change came swiftly, racing through his body to break bones and reform them in new lengths and angles. His skin tingled as fur replaced flesh. A quick stab of pain accompanied each claw and fang that erupted from his skin, but soon his world changed to amber as his wolf vision took over. He raced by his brothers, bumping into Raine and knocking him off his feet. Pete's laughter at Raine's expense followed him as he loped into the underbrush.

* * * *

Raine didn't like breaking his word. But he hadn't agreed. He hadn't said he'd stay away from Callie. Still, he wouldn't like it if his brothers ditched him like he planned to do to them.

But he couldn't help it. He'd had a difficult time staying off her on the walk back to camp. But when Pete had arrived with her sweet fragrance on him, an aroma that reminded him of cinnamon rolls, he thought he'd go crazy. He'd never know how he'd managed to keep from running to her and throwing her to the floor of their tent. Now his restraint was shattered and he had no choice but to listen to his lust.

Slowing his pace, he let his brothers take the lead. That wasn't unusual for him to do so. He often let them charge ahead on a run. At times, when another trail or the scent of another animal touched his nostrils, he'd take off on his own.

Blue surged ahead as he always did with Pete doing his best to keep up. They'd get so immersed in competing against each other that they'd never miss him. He slowed down again, putting even more distance between them. Then, as they turned a corner, he slammed to a stop, spun around, and headed back to camp.

He was back and standing at the edge of the forest when the first drops of rain fell. Shifting, he took his human form again then snatched up his clothes he'd left there. Checking around to see if anyone was watching, he hurried on bare feet to the entrance of the tent.

What if she's asleep?

He hadn't thought about that. Would he frighten her by coming in without warning? Especially if he startled her out of her dreams?

I wonder if she's having wet dreams.

His cock twitched to life. He'd make sure she had a wet dream after he was through with her.

He brought forth his wolf's sensitive hearing, stirring the animal inside him again. But he wouldn't let it take control. Not while he was with her. The sound of steady breathing was all he heard.

I wonder if she's dreaming about me.

"Can I go home now?"

He almost jumped out of his skin at the sound of Luke's voice. The big guy, a werebear of considerable size even for one of them, rambled toward him from around the back of the tent. He put his fingers to his lips, warning Luke to get quiet.

"I forgot you were watching her." His whisper was husky and filled with the lust inside him.

Luke's brow knitted. "Yup. Is it okay to leave? Lyra's waiting on me."

"Sure. Go ahead. I'll take it from here. And thanks."

"Yup." Luke jerked his head up and down, then pivoted and headed in the direction of his teepee. Although a teepee wasn't the usual style of home for a shifter, much less a werebear, Lyra had chosen their home in deference to her Native American culture. That and because shape-shifters like her liked that a teepee was easy to break down and put up in a different location.

He waited until Luke had gone into his teepee before pushing through the flaps of the tent. Only a couple of candles remained lit, but his eyes adjusted easily going from the darkness outside to the interior of the tent.

He found her, curled into a ball near the back of the tent. Unlike many of the other werewolves, they'd kept the tent as one large open area instead of using quilts and other materials to section off parts into smaller rooms. He crossed the open area and gazed down at her.

Her dark hair spread out behind her as though a strong breeze was blowing it away from her body. Her eyelashes feathered her cheekbones and pointed toward the full lips that were slightly parted. A rose hue colored her skin and her breaths came in a soft, even rhythm. She had one of the quilts pulled over her body, but her bare shoulder peeked out from underneath the material.

How does she get more beautiful every time I see her?

He tugged off his clothes, careful to keep quiet. If he was going to wake her, then he'd bring her out of her sleep in a very special way.

Kneeling beside her, he touched her cheek with a gentle stroke of the back of his fingers. She moaned and stirred, then rolled over on her back. The tip of one breast slipped out from under the quilt.

His gaze fell on her, taking in the brown tint of her areola. Her nipple was already taut and he wondered if it was due to the chill or from his touch. She was the perfect size for him to cup in the palm of his hand. He could already feel the soft give of her skin as he squeezed it.

Would she get angry at him for watching her while she slept? Or would she get turned on?

If she woke up and wanted him to stop, would he have the strength to do as she asked? Or would his desire for her mixed with his inner wolf howling at him to take her be too much to resist?

Either way, he had to find out.

He leaned over and flicked the tip of his tongue over her nipple. She moaned and he paused, waiting to see if she'd open her eyes. When she didn't, he did it again as he reached up and held her other nipple between his fingers. Her nipples hardened even more. His cock twitched to life, growing large in only a few seconds.

He sat back and removed his hand. He flattened his hands on his knees, keeping them there as a form of delicious torture. How much sweeter would it be to touch her after not doing so? But his resistance was too low to hold out for long.

Taking the hem of the quilt, he tugged it, bringing it down her flat stomach to stop at her waist. She was naked. At least from what he'd seen so far. Only then did he see a dress lying on a nearby quilt along with a pair of moccasins. He guessed that Lyra had brought her a fresh change of clothing and had more than likely taken her other clothes to wash for her. He reminded himself to thank Luke's mate. Callie was a sexy sight in her jeans and T-shirt, but he'd bet she'd look even better in the simple dress. Just thinking about sliding his hand under the soft material and finding her without panties made his cock grow bigger.

She mumbled something under her breath that even his sensitive hearing couldn't pick up. Then, to his delight, she kicked the quilt off.

Her beauty lay before him. Long, silky legs spread apart as she squirmed in her sleep. Her mons was covered with dark curly hair that led to the pretty folds of her skin. Moisture glistened there, beckoning to him to take a drink.

Yet again he tormented himself. Instead of taking the drink he wanted, he leaned over her and rained soft kisses over her breasts. Again, he squeezed her softness as he bit and teased her other nipple. She arched higher now, tempting him more.

He glanced upward. Was she still asleep? Her eyes remained closed.

His strong hand covered her mons and she moaned her encouragement. He responded, slipping his finger between her folds. If she wasn't asleep, she was playing his game.

Keeping one hand on her breast to hold her nipple to his mouth, he let his other hand work elsewhere. He bent her knee, then slid his hand to the wetness between her legs.

He moaned, sliding his tongue from one breast to the other. Heat raced through him, hotter than he could ever remember it happening. Her legs fell open for him and again he checked her face for any sign that she was only pretending to sleep. He pressed his large cock against her pussy, making him ache to shove it inside her.

His hands roamed her body, exploring every curve, every swell, every inch of her. She whimpered and sent the sweet rush of yearning scorching through him. His cock moved as though with a mind of its own.

Now was the moment of decision and he made it. If she was the one for them, she'd want this. If not, and she woke up infuriated, he'd leave and never bother her again.

You're a damn animal.

A growl rumbled from deep inside in answer.

Yes, I am and damn proud of it.

He froze as the thought struck him. For the first time in his life he had to wonder if being a werewolf was a good thing. What if she wanted him and his brothers as men, but couldn't accept the animal side of them? But then, if she couldn't, didn't that mean she wasn't the one for them after all?

But all that would have to wait. Right now, he had to taste her.

Sliding over her, he took in the swell of her breasts and the perfect amount of cleavage they formed. Her breasts stood upright, small but perky. He could see the muscles in her stomach. Not overly ripped, but just the right amount that left a small round mound just before leading to her mons.

He held his face over her pussy and drank in the sight of her. She mewled, and, as though she really knew he was there, spread her legs wider. He lay down between them then, taking care to be very gentle, urged her folds apart. The wondrous aroma of her wafted over him and made the wolf inside scratch to come to the surface. She was pink, pretty, and perfect. She was, simply put, the most beautiful sight he'd ever seen.

Doing the only thing any man could've done, he flicked his tongue over her clit. She trembled, her hands clutching the quilt beneath her. Her taste was unique, reminding him of the sweet nectar of honey in a hive with an added splash of spiciness he couldn't define. He slid his hands under her buttocks and pulled her to him. Pressing his mouth to her pussy, he sucked in her clit.

She gasped, stilled, then lifted a leg and kicked him in the shoulder. "What the—"

Chapter Five

"Ow!"

Callie jerked to a sitting position and kicked Raine again.

"Hey, knock it off. It's me, Raine."

She glared at him, but the glare soon turned into astonishment when her gaze dropped from his face to his oh-so-long cock. Lust pummeled her like a freight train on a runaway rail. His cock was large and curved to a bulbous end just like Pete's.

"Callie."

She wanted to yell at him, to demand what he thought he was doing, but the way he said her name changed her mind. Instead, she reached out to him and took him by his hair. "Don't stop now."

His chuckle was muffled as she forced his head between her legs. He tugged her legs over his shoulders and pulled her to him. His mouth on her clit sent her flying and she bucked, at once wanting to get away from the delicious agony and bring it closer. She clutched her breasts, felt the wetness on her nipples, and wished she'd been awake to experience the pleasure he'd given them.

He'd wanted to awaken her with sex and he had—the same way she'd always wanted a man to do. His hands slid under her buttocks, kneading the fleshy mounds and clinging to her. He added a finger then another to her pussy and pumped her. But when he found her G-spot, she was putty in his hands. She cried out as an orgasm took hold and flew her along with it.

Nibbling, sucking, he pleasured her. She quivered under his touch as the rush of another climax roared free. He lifted her and sucked on her clit harder as he plunged his fingers inside. She gasped, clutching the quilt to keep her anchored to the ground. As soon as a climax would finish its shuddering ride through her body, he'd give her a moment to regroup then dive in to eat her again.

Her mind spun as the tension inside her whipped into high gear yet again. Thunder reverberated through the floor as lightning flashed, brightening the tent and adding to the storm swirling inside her. She reached for him, unable to take much more.

"Please, Raine. Now."

He slid his tongue over her mons, then along the swell of her stomach, stopping to tease her with a kiss to her belly button. "Now what? Should I leave you alone so you can go back to sleep?" The look in his eyes teased her.

She growled at him and reached for his arms. Yet instead of shoving the cock that pressed against her pussy, the cock that she ached for, inside her, he took her under the arms and pulled her on top of his lap. He laughed at her yelp of surprise, and, enclosing her in his strong arm, he took her breast and brought her taut nipple to his mouth. His hard cock pushed against her, rubbing against her, challenging her to take control.

She lifted up, took his cock in her hand and plunged downward. His groan mixed with hers as he drove deep inside her. She swore she could feel the end of him nearing her belly button and ground her hips against him harder. But that was her imagination, just as she was imagining that his eyes had turned amber for a split second. Yet as soon as she'd looked again to check, they were back to their normal color.

Lightning flashed and thunder clapped, the boom resonating through the tent like a living creature as he entered her, driving into her wetness. She bucked in sync with him, riding him, imploring him to go deeper and to thrust harder than the time before. He growled, a low, animal-like sound, and, when she gazed into his eyes, she thought she saw the blue change to amber again. She answered the only way she could by clutching his neck and bringing his mouth to her tit.

Pumping upward into her, he murmured words she never thought she'd hear. Words of tenderness, of love, and even of commitment. She cried out his name, giving him a tribute to his lovemaking and more. Her heart opened to let him in, even as her mind warned her to take care.

As the storm raged outside, they reached their climaxes together and screamed their pleasure into the night.

Thunder rumbled far away as their bodies quivered together. She held him, her arms around him, his forehead resting against her shoulder. Neither made an attempt to slide his cock out of her, and if he wanted to stay that way for the rest of the night she'd let him.

Or we could do it all over again.

She smiled, pressing her mouth to his shoulder to give him a tender kiss. He moaned a satisfied sound, then echoed her kiss with one of his own.

He wiped the perspiration away from her brow. "You're beautiful, you know. And sexy as hell."

"Prove it."

His eyes widened in surprise. "Okay, I will. But give me a little time, okay? I'm not a sex machine."

"You could've fooled me."

He laid her back, coming to rest at her side. "So I take it that it was okay for me to do what I did?"

She loved the way he skimmed his fingertip from one nipple to the other. They had remained at attention, ready for more action. "If you mean waking me up with sex, then yeah, it was okay."

"Maybe even better than okay?"

Give the man an inch... Wait. He already has quite a few inches.

"Oh, hell, yeah. Much better than okay."

"I know this isn't the right thing to say, but I've got to know. For no other reason than bragging rights."

She played with his lower lip with her thumb. "Bragging rights?"

"Yeah. So which of us is better? Pete or me?"

She lifted up and rested her head on her hand. "Are you seriously asking me that?"

He tried to backpedal as fast as he could. "Uh, judging from the look on your face, I'd like to retract my question."

She sat up, suddenly aware of the implications. "Is that what this is? Is that what Blue meant by using the term *ours*? Are you three in a competition to see who can get the stupid girl who fell into a hole in the sack?"

He was on his feet two seconds after she was. "What? No. It was just a stupid question. You saw how we are, always ribbing each other. I…Oh, hell, I don't know why I asked it."

She grabbed one of the quilts and covered her body. "I don't care why you asked it either. Just get the hell out. Tell Blue he lost since he didn't screw me. As for you and Pete, why don't you yank out your dicks and see which one can piss the longest, because I'm not calling a winner."

"Callie, you've got it all wrong."

She punched him in the chest and he acted like he didn't even notice. She didn't have a chance of keeping them off her if they wanted her.

"Is that the whole contest? Or was tying me up part of it?" She thrust out her arms, putting her wrists together. "Here. Go ahead and do it again. Tie me up and do whatever perverted shit you want to me. Let's get this captor-fucks-the-captive game over with so I can go home."

He stared at her as though she'd gone crazy. And maybe she had. Tears burned behind her eyes, but she'd be damned if she'd let him see her cry. It was her own fault for letting him, them, get close to her. She'd even thought for a brief moment that maybe, just maybe she could have something special with one or even all of them.

Shit. My heart hurts. It really, truly hurts.

She clutched her fist to her chest and thrust her other hand toward the flaps of the tent. "Please. Leave me alone."

"Callie, please, let me explain. You are ours. But not in the way you think. This isn't a game."

"It's always a game." *A game I always lose.*

She couldn't look at him. If she did, she might be dumb enough to believe him. Instead, she turned away and kept her back straight. "Get out."

Once she heard the rustle of the flaps and the sound of him moving away in the darkness, she let the tears slide down her cheeks. She was such a fool. How could she have opened her heart so wide in such a short time? She knew better than to trust anyone with her heart.

But I thought they were...Were what? Special? The "one" three times over? When did I start believing in that shit?

Yet the answer was clear enough. She hadn't been aware of it, but she'd started believing the moment she'd looked into their eyes.

She threw herself down on a pile of quilts and sobbed.

* * * *

"Callie?"

She whirled around at the sound of Blue's voice. Going against everything she'd told herself since Raine had gone the night before, she let the rush of emotions fill her.

It's sexual attraction, that's all.

Yet the dull ache in the middle of her stomach said otherwise. Blue's enticing blue gaze stole her breath away. He was clothed in the same light-colored pants Luke had worn along with moccasins like the ones she had on. The dress she'd found in the tent was comfortable, although going without any underwear was taking a bit of getting used to. She could've changed into the extra set of clothing she had in her pack, but the dress had looked so tempting that she hadn't been able to resist.

"Are you here to take me back down the mountain?" She was glad she could muster up an angry tone. After figuring out what they had in mind, each of them planning to add a notch to their belts, she didn't owe him civility.

The lightness in his features faded. "No."

"Really. Well, if that's too far, then you could show me back to the pit. I think I could find my way back to a place where I could get my bearings. I could take it from there."

"I can't do that, either."

Fear curled its way into her like a snake slithering across the ground and wiped her anger away. "Why not?"

He pulled one side of the opening flaps back and inclined his head toward the outside. "Come on. Take a walk with me and I'll try to explain."

After last night's revelation with Raine, she wasn't in the mood for any explanations. She wanted results, but in order to get them she had to play along. "Fine. But you'd better do more than try. And no funny business, either." She stalked past him.

Damn, but he smells good.

Not in the way most men she knew smelled good. His wasn't an aroma that came from expensive aftershave. His came from his skin, his breath, and his very being.

It doesn't matter how good he smells. Keep your guard up.

"It's Kirkland."

"What?"

"My last name. It's Kirkland."

She wasn't sure why, but suddenly she wanted him to know.

He smiled. "Callie Kirkland. I like it. It fits you."

He followed her into the sunlight then stopped as she came to a standstill. The sight around her was amazing, throwing all other concerns out of her mind. The people she'd seen last night were back, along with many others. Children of all ages dashed about, playing and shouting at their friends, then laughing as women tried to corral them. At last, one very large woman with a long braid of red hair bouncing down her spine gathered them together and herded them into the woods. A couple of other women along with three men followed them, disappearing into the heavy brush.

"Where are they going?"

"Who?

She pointed in the direction that the children had gone. "The kids. Why are they taking them into the forest?"

Blue took her hand and she couldn't bring herself to remove it from his. "They're taking them on a nature walk so they can learn about the medicinal purposes of the plants."

"So it's like a community school? Or homeschooling?"

Luke ambled by with two other large men who, judging by their size and their similar features, had to be relatives. He lifted his hand in greeting and she did the same. "Are those Luke's brothers?"

"Yup."

She smirked at Blue's imitation of the way Luke talked. Checking around her, she found several groups of men and women who appeared to be related. "Is that common? The brother thing?"

"For us, yes. We tend to stick with family. But there are others who join together to make new families." He took the orange a small woman with flowing blonde hair gave him, thanked her, then started pulling it apart.

Callie took the wedge he offered her. "What's this place called? Have you always lived here? Or is this one of those retreats people pay exorbitant amounts of money to visit? Is it a getting-back-to-nature therapeutic resort?"

"I'll tell you what you want to know, but you have to promise me that you'll keep an open mind."

"You people sure do ask for a lot of promises." She paused to stare at a man whose nose was very wide. Long teeth jutted out over his bottom lip. He stretched his lips wide, exposing more teeth, and making her aware that she was gaping at him. She looked away, embarrassed by her rudeness. But then it hit her. Many of the people around her were unique in their appearance. Some had large teeth or facial features while others seemed different in their coloring or the way they held themselves.

"I just want to make sure you don't jump the gun and think I'm crazy."

Crazy? Her interest piqued. "This sounds interesting."

"We call our home The Hidden."

"Right. Lyra told me that."

He gave her a short glance. "What else did she tell you?"

"Not much. She said you Deacon boys should be the ones to explain."

"Then I'd better get on with it. The Hidden is our sanctuary."

He paused to take a bite of the orange and she took one, too. Juice ran down her hand and the sweet taste erupted in her mouth. "Wow. That's a really good orange. I think it's the best one I've ever had."

"The fruit in The Hidden is a lot better than on The Outside."

"The Outside?" Not caring if it was unladylike, she shoved the rest of her piece into her mouth and sighed as the delicious flavor spread over her tongue and down her throat.

"That's what we call everything outside of here." He gestured toward a group of people sharing a meal and laughing. "You may have noticed that some of the people here are a bit different."

She nodded then opened her hand palm up to ask for another slice of orange. He gave it to her and started walking again, taking long strides that made her hustle to keep up with him. All the while, she tried not to stare at those around her.

"That's why they're here. Because of their differences, they can get hassled elsewhere. Plus, this place is special. It's serene and the weather's always wonderful." He drew her in with his intense look. "You'll see things in The Hidden that you'll never see anywhere else in the world."

"You're making this place sound almost magical."

A hint of a smile formed on his lips. "'Magical' is a good word for

The Hidden."

"So tell me how you and your brothers found this place. I know for a fact that I've never heard of it or seen it on any map. I studied maps of the region before I came hiking."

"That's why it's called The Hidden. We want to keep it a secret." He said hello to a couple of men who passed by. "Raine and I are natives, believe it or not. Our parents came here before we were born. Then they took in Pete and made him our brother."

He tossed the rind of the orange into the bushes. "But I'm more interested in hearing how you fell into that pit."

She winced. "I hope I can live that catastrophe down."

"It's not that bad. Everyone trips and falls at some point. And you had an extra reason to get careless with the buck chasing you. But did anything else happen?"

"I saw that weird creature, then three wolves. Then that's when you showed up." Why did she have the impression that he was fishing for something else?

"But did you see, or maybe feel, anything out of the ordinary?"

She was right. He was searching for answers. "Yeah. I did. When the buck was chasing me—Pete said its name is Jerry—I ran like hell. But then it was like I hit an invisible wall. One second, I was going full steam ahead and then, all of sudden, it felt like I was trying to run through water. I could feel this substance that was heavier than air rippling around me."

She gave him a suspicious look. "Do you know what I'm talking about?"

His answer seemed sincere enough. "No. I've never experienced that."

"So do you guys do that a lot?"

He blinked, thrown by her switching the subject. "Do what?"

"Name the animals. Like calling that buck Jerry."

"Yeah, we kind of do."

"Like pets?"

A flash of irritation swept over his features. "We don't have pets because we don't think any living being should own another."

Touchy subject, huh? She decided not to push him.

"Tell me about the creature. Lyra knew what I was talking about and you do, too. I can see that you do."

"They're called The Cursed because of their ugly appearance. And they're dangerous. Stay away from them and stay inside the camp area, especially after dark."

"I've never heard of them, much less seen one before."

"Like I said"—he took her hand again and gripped it harder—"stay in the camp."

"I'm not planning on staying at all."

"And here's where the open mind part comes in."

"Uh-oh. I don't like the sound of that."

He started walking again, pulling her along with him, and led her onto a narrow path leading into the forest. The sunlight dimmed as it struggled to get through the tree limbs. Animals scurried away and into the underbrush. Brilliantly colored flowers lined the path.

If any place is magical, this place is.

"Where are we going?"

"We're meeting my brothers at the pond." He picked up his pace even more and she had to jog to keep up.

"Do you remember the white-haired man you saw last night?"

"Sure. He was with the little guy that reminded me of an elf." She hissed at her mistake. "I'm sorry. That was so un-PC of me. I can't believe I said that."

"Don't worry about it. Titto wouldn't mind. Anyway, the older man is Charlton and he heads up The Council. They're the ones who determine the rules around here. What few we have, that is."

"And?" She tensed up, expecting the worst.

"The Council has determined that you should stay a few days until we can sort things out."

She froze. "And what if I don't want to?"

"I'm sorry, Callie. That's the way it has to be."

He pulled her along with him until they broke through the tree line and to the edge of a beautiful pool of water. Even from where she was standing, several feet from it, she could see through the clear blue liquid to the bottom. Fish whipped about with one popping to the surface every once in a while.

Raine and Pete stood in the shallow part. Her heart picked up speed, almost forgetting what Blue had told her.

Holy crap. They're naked.

* * * *

Blue could see the yearning on her face, but he could also see her hesitation. But he couldn't blame her. Not after Raine told them what had happened last night. He'd almost lost control with his brothers. Both Pete and Raine had already lain with her—which drove him crazy—but not only had Raine done so, he'd done it after they'd agreed to leave her alone.

"Don't worry, Callie. Nothing's going to happen." He couldn't keep from running his gaze over her and imagining her body skimming through the water, her long hair trailing behind her. "Unless you want it to."

Her response was swift and filled with anger. "Sorry. You're shit out of luck. I'm not giving you the green light so you can complete the challenge, or game, or whatever the hell you guys want to call it."

"That's not what's going on here."

"Then why don't you tell me what is going on?"

Although she was angry, her words spoken in a challenge, he could sense the longing inside her. She wanted to hear that she was wrong, yearned to believe what he'd tell her was the truth.

"I don't know how to explain it well. You're going to have to listen to your gut and recognize that what I'm saying is real." He stepped closer to her, needing to touch her as though his touch would succeed where his words had failed. But she stayed out of his reach.

"There's a special something happening between us. Between all four of us."

Her anger diminished, but her knitted brow told him she wasn't ready to accept everything he'd said. If she believed him enough to know that they weren't playing games with her, then that'd be okay. For now.

"Do you trust us?" He stopped her with his palm up and facing her. "No, don't answer yet. And don't listen to your head. Listen to your heart. Then answer." He paused, giving her time to do as he'd asked. "Do you trust us?"

"Yes. I think so."

"Then believe me when I say this is not a game to us. Can you do that?"

She narrowed her eyes and he could almost see her mind warring with her heart. "Yes. I think I can."

"Good. Then let's have a little fun, okay?"

He paced to a large tree, reached out behind it, and brought out her backpack. "Pete brought this along."

"Does that mean I can leave?" She took the bag from him and opened it to examine the contents.

Did she think they'd stolen her stuff? That and the way she'd glared at him cut him to the bone. He had a lot to make up to her, but, if he had his way, he'd have a lifetime to do it.

"No."

She pulled herself taller. "And what if I take off right now?"

"I'll have to stop you any way I can."

"So I'm still a prisoner. Are you planning on tying me up again?"

"Only if you want me to." If she said yes, he'd grab the first thing he could to tie her up, then strip her clothes off. His wolf howled with delight as he pictured her, bound, lying on the green grass at his feet.

Her eyes flashed before she took a step back. "Don't even think about it. Can I at least take some photos? Or is that not allowed, too?"

"Sure. Go ahead." Whatever pictures she took would never leave The Hidden. He would make certain of that.

"And I'll be your first subject."

He pivoted along with her to face a very wet and very aroused Raine. The sweet scent of lust flowed off her, cocooning him until he thought he'd lose his mind. His wolf roared again, howling at her nearness and demanding that he answer the call of the wild.

She opened to her mouth to speak, closed it, then tried again. "Okay. Yeah. Why not? At least that way I can keep my eye on you."

"How about me? I'm better looking than this fugly dude." Pete shoved Raine out of the way and struck a pose.

Blue was relieved to see her smile, but it was gone all too soon. Maybe, just maybe he could get that smile back. He tugged off his shirt as he toed off his boots. "How about a threesome?"

Shit!

"Sorry. I didn't mean that kind of threesome. Just three men to shoot." He knew he shouldn't, but he couldn't resist. "Unless you want a foursome instead."

Was it just wishful thinking, or did she almost accept his offer? But her mouth slammed shut as she regrouped. "Foursome, no? About shooting you? Don't I wish. But I'm sorry to say I don't have a gun."

Pete covered his junk with both hands. "Ow. And here I was going to ask you to make sure you got my best feature in the photo."

Again, her face softened a little more. They were making inroads to lighten her anger. She pulled the camera from the backpack and checked it, making sure things were ready. "You three are something else."

"Which makes us perfect for you."

Blue bumped his shoulder against Raine's. "You got the wrong impression from him last night, but he's dead-on right now."

"Will everyone stop talking about shooting something? Little Pete's having a hard time staying up."

Blue jumped at the opening and struck a pose right out of a

clothing catalogue. "Take my picture first, Callie."

She lifted the camera and aimed. He heard the click, but she didn't act happy when she lowered the camera and looked to Raine then Pete. "I still have to know. Why did you do that? Why did you sleep with me? Was it to have fun with a girl you knew wasn't going to hang around for long? Or did you think I owed you for helping me? I know you don't know me—"

"We know enough." Blue hoped she could see the truth on his face.

"I know I shouldn't have hopped into the sack with you guys, but...I thought it was...real."

Raine moved forward, but Blue held him back. She needed her space. "I thought you said you believed me. They—we—were never playing a game."

"What I said and did was straight from the heart," added Pete. "As I'm sure it was for Raine."

Raine chimed in. "It's true, Callie. You've got us all wrong."

"So you're saying it was more than just sex?"

She was vulnerable and he could smell it drifting off her. "I haven't gotten the honor of lying with you yet, but I know it was a lot more than that for them."

He wanted to hold her, to reassure her with his touch as well as his words, but she wasn't ready. Instead, he'd have to make his words count like never before. If he had to say it a thousand times to reassure her, he would.

"This is hard to believe even for us, and I know it's got to be even harder for you to accept. But, Callie, you're the woman we've waited for."

She shook her head, denying his words. But her open expression told him she wanted to trust him. "We only met yesterday."

"It doesn't matter," Pete whispered, but his tone carried as though he'd howled the words.

Pete glanced at him, but Blue waved him back. No matter how

hard it was to keep away from her, that's what they had to do. For now. But his inner wolf, scratching to take over, didn't like it any better than he did.

"That's how it is with us. When we meet the woman who's supposed to be our mate, then we know. Sometimes in an instant, but other times it takes a little longer." He grinned. "Even a whole day."

She shot him a doubtful look. "So I'm the woman for all three of you?"

He finally took that step forward and was relieved when she didn't tell him to stay where he was. "You are."

"That's not possible."

Did he hear yearning in her voice? "It is. I've seen it. You can ask people back at camp. For us, it happens that way."

"For us? What does that mean?"

He couldn't tell her they were werewolves. Not until she accepted the possibility that she was meant for them. "Tell me you haven't felt anything for us above and beyond the physical."

She couldn't and she wouldn't. He had to believe that even if she didn't trust him yet, her gut would tell her the truth.

"Is that why I can't leave right now?"

"Yes."

Raine shifted back and forth on his feet and Pete cleared his throat. Blue could sense the beasts inside them, pacing, waiting. Like him, they knew there were more reasons, but wasn't love the most important one? The fact that it wasn't The Time for Leaving or that they weren't sure if the portal was still there didn't matter. All that mattered was getting her to trust them and to realize she belonged with them.

"So? Are we doing a photo shoot or what?"

"Yeah, Blue. We are. Pete, move onto that rock over there."

She'd decided to accept what they'd said for now. But he knew she'd want a better explanation later. She'd need time to process the information he'd thrown at her, yet compared to other women he'd heard about, she was handling it well.

He motioned to Pete to get going. Pete clambered on top of the flat rock and stretched out, his cock erect and flying.

"How's this?"

She clicked a photo then hurried to another position to take one more. "Perfect. And you're okay with my showing these photos off? Would you be all right with my putting them in an exhibit? Maybe to sell?"

Pete's eyebrows shot up. "I guess. But you have to promise me something."

Blue almost laughed when she puffed out her exasperation.

"What is it with you guys and promises? Now what do I have to promise?"

"You have to swear you won't get jealous. Once you show the photos of me to your girlfriends, they're going to want to know where to find me. You make sure you tell them that I'm a one-woman man and that you're the one woman."

He should've told his brother to stop pushing, but when he saw her hesitation and when she didn't answer, he couldn't help but feel encouraged.

Pete sat up and flexed his muscles. "Is this a good pose?"

Before she could answer, Raine jumped on top of the rock and pushed Pete off. He yelped as he fell to the ground and Callie laughed. Blue dashed past them and into the pool as Callie regrouped and started taking more shots.

"Let's get all three of you in the water." She waved her arm, directing his brothers to join him. They posed, Raine and Pete with their backs to Blue, who stood in the middle with his hands clasped behind his back.

* * * *

Callie didn't know what to think. Did she believe what Blue had told her? She couldn't, could she? Every time she'd let her guard down, trusting in people who'd made promises to her, she'd always ended up getting hurt. Did she dare let the men into her heart? They were different, but was what they'd told her real?

She was afraid to take that risk, but a part of her ached to do so. Was that because this was the one time her heart wouldn't get hurt? If she could believe, would she finally gain the love and the home she'd wanted her entire life? Wasn't that worth the risk?

Could they love her so fast? Did she care for them?

She'd never been one of those girls who thought her white knight would arrive to make her life complete. And love at first sight? That bullshit was for hopeless romantics.

Wasn't it?

Her mind whirled and her heart ached, needing answers to her questions. But taking the photos helped. Not only did it take her mind off what he'd told her, leaving it for later when she was alone and could think it through, but it was giving her shots any other woman photographer, professional or amateur, would kill for.

Wow, but they're amazing.

She'd taken pictures of bodybuilders, models, and actors, men who made it their profession to look good, but the Deacon brothers put them to shame. Their muscles glistened as the droplets of water coasted down their hard chests and ripped stomachs. The water reached their lean waists, but she could still see their hard cocks through the clear water. Each was lined with blue-purple veins and capped with a bulbous end that begged her to lick it. Raine's and Pete's cocks were curved, but she doubted Blue's would fail to find her sweet spot. She almost regretted her sexual romps with Pete and Raine because she hadn't taken the time to feast on their cocks.

I'll make sure I suck them the next time.

She paused, then went straight into the next shot as the men turned and gave her their backs to admire. They had the broadest shoulders she'd ever seen and her fingers itched to slide over their skin. Or to pinch their firm, round asses.

The next time?

If it were up to the Deacon men, there'd be a next time. But did she want that?

Hell, yeah.

She bit her lip. After giving them hell when she thought they were playing a sex game with her, now she was ready for more. Was she a hypocrite? Or was it her turn to choose the game?

Again, she felt the yearning to believe them. If they'd really fallen for her, could she refuse them? She'd be a fool not to want them. Her mouth watered at the idea.

She stopped, letting herself feel more than think the answers to the questions that could change her life forever.

Do I trust them? Yes.

Do I believe them? Yes.

Do I care for them?

The part of her that had been hurt so many times before tried to tell her to keep herself safe, to not fall victim to another lie. She swallowed, her nerves threatening to send her into flight mode again. But when her gaze fell on the men again, she had her answer.

Yes. As crazy as it is, I do care for them. How the hell did that happen?

She smiled, her nerves settling as the warmth that filled her heart overtook all her doubts.

Who cares how as long as it did?

"Guys, go over there by the waterfall."

They did as she asked, pushing and shoving each other to get the best position. She liked how one minute they acted like men and then, in the next, they were three boys roughhousing with each other.

"Let the waterfall run over your bodies."

They treaded water, but managed to keep their shoulders above the surface. Moving under the stream, they did their best to strike poses that were straight out of a sex magazine. She held the camera up and started taking pictures.

Holy hell. I couldn't have found three more delectable-looking men if I'd ordered them for Christmas.

Blue closed his eyes and held back his head. Running his palms over his shaved head made his arms flex and he opened his mouth, closed his eyes, and adopted an expression that had her pussy clenching with need.

Is that what his face looks like when he comes?

She trembled. Didn't she want to find out?

Hell, yeah, I do.

Raine reached up and copied his brother. But instead of opening his mouth and closing his eyes, he stared straight at her. The animalistic glint in his eyes made her fumble with the camera. His biceps jumped as he put on a wicked smile.

Or is it triceps? Whichever it is, he's fucking sexy as hell.

Pete rubbed his chest, pretending to wash himself as he tossed quick glances at her. Water coursed over their bodies as the mist from the splashes formed a haze around them.

These photos are going to be awesome.

But she wanted even more. "Okay, I've got it. Come back out of the water and get close to the trees."

They came out of the pool, like a trio of Poseidons. Water ran down their long limbs and made sparkling highlights against their tanned skin. She watched, entranced as they lined up with the woods as their background.

Her mouth watered and she licked her lips. Daring to make the move, she lowered the camera and let out a long breath. "Stroke your cocks."

"What?"

"You heard me, Raine. Pleasure yourselves."

They took a moment to check with each other then took their cocks in their hands. "Okay, boys. Let's show her what we've got."

"Yeah. Like Pete said. Give me your best."

Blue began slowly, all the while keeping his eyes on her. He slid his hand along his length and leaned against a tree.

Raine was more in a hurry. He cupped his balls with one hand while he pumped his cock. Groaning, he planted his feet apart and faced directly forward.

She squinted into the camera. Was it the light, or did all of them have bits of amber in their eyes? She'd seen it before, but it wasn't important to ask what it was right now. Hell, she was surprised that she could even think with them in their naked-and-beyond-gorgeous states.

She clicked off several pictures before pointing the camera toward Pete. He had his back against a tree like Blue and jerked his cock. Placing his other hand in front of his cock, he worked his hips back and forth, jabbing into his palm.

Sweat broke out along her hairline. Her thoughts jumbled together, refusing to think as she watched them work their dicks.

"This would be a lot more fun if you'd join us."

"Shut up, Pete. She needs time," admonished Blue.

Think.

But it was only her body talking now. A primal urge deep inside her had awakened, taking control, making the rush of powerful sensations ride her along its wave. She started forward, her mouth watering as she wondered what they'd taste like. Then, as the idea came to her, she stopped and lowered the camera to the ground.

"Stay."

Swaying as seductively as she could, she walked over to the rock the men had posed on and climbed up. She faced them, the heat from the flat surface no match for the heat already firing her body. Giving them a sultry look, she pulled the skirt of her dress to her waist.

As one, they gaped at her. When Raine took a step her way, she held up her hand. "I said stay."

They'd tied her up and told her to stay where she was, denying her the right to leave. But now it was her turn to make demands.

The longing she saw in their eyes was almost enough to break her resolve. But she had another idea in mind. Tossing her hair back, she slid her hand between her legs and found her wet pussy.

"Aw, hell. She's torturing us." Pete quickened his hand.

"Payback is a bitch, you know." Yet when she took her hand away, Raine hurriedly added, "I'm not calling you a bitch. Shit. You know what I mean."

"I sure do." She put her hand back then lay back as she pulled her folds apart. "Ooh, I'm so nice and pink. And wet."

Blue groaned as she thrust a finger into her pussy then pulled it out and sucked it dry. "You're killing me."

"Us. She's killing us, man," added Raine.

She stroked herself, rubbing her middle finger over her throbbing clit. Thinking of how Raine had awakened her, with his tongue on her, she sped up, going faster until she was panting with the effort.

Damn, how I want to fuck them.

But playing her game was best for now. "Harder, Blue. I want to see your cum shooting out."

He did as she wanted, his face a mask of determination. "Tell me I'm going to get to fuck you."

She chuckled. "I'll think about it." Lifting one eyebrow, she added, "Maybe I'll let all three of you have me at the same time. Would you like that, guys?"

"It's what we want most."

Pete's hungry tone surprised her.

She gave them a look that promised everything, yet teased that she might take it away in the next moment. She wanted them as much as they wanted her, but she would decide how and when.

For the first time in her life, she trusted herself enough to trust someone else completely.

They wanted her alone and together. She mewled as a small orgasm sprang free. Having the three Deacon brothers licking, biting, sucking on her as she took their cocks was beyond comprehension.

She circled her finger over and around her clit as she slid her hand under the top of her dress to pinch her nipple. Sounds of need and desire surrounded her and she realized that her own voice added to the mix.

Pete's mouth was slack as he pumped his cock. Pre-cum oozed from the tip, and again, she imagined how it would taste. Raine's expression was similar as he worked his cock, his climax drawing near. Blue's face, on the other hand, was set and determined as though he were trying to hold on for as long as he could.

She pushed her finger against the hard nub between the tiny folds and moved her hand as fast as she could. The first small orgasm she'd had was only the beginning and the turmoil inside her was barreling frantically toward the end. Keeping her nipple between her two fingers, she twisted it and longed to have one of the men's teeth giving her the pain.

Pete groaned, the grounded-out sound changing to a roar as he came. His cum shot out, falling to the green forest floor. Seconds later, Raine cried out and his body jerked out his release. Blue held on, but his face was growing tighter, heralding his fading control.

"Do you want me, Blue?"

He groaned, his features tightening more. "Hell, yeah."

"But you can't have me. Not yet." She felt more powerful and in control than she had since she'd fallen into the pit. Than she ever had. Didn't that alone prove that they were right for her? That she was truly meant for them? Their love freed her from all the horrible things she'd gone through in her life. At last, she was truly free.

"Until then, I want to see you come. Come for me, Blue."

She wanted to hold back and have him come first, but when she saw that he was about to let loose, she came with him, their shouts mingling in the air and sending birds into flight. Their moans grew softer with each new tremble.

She scanned from one man to the next then back again, unable to get her fill. Next time, she'd do more than watch. Blue slumped against the tree while Raine and Pete, spent, went to their knees.

Closing her eyes, she let the warmth of the sun wash over her.

Maybe I'll go swimming with them.

Yet when she opened her eyes, her voice caught in her throat.

There it is.

Chapter Six

The creature she'd seen before—his white diamond a distinct contrast to the black of his face—was hiding in the woods behind the men. If they hadn't been so absorbed in pleasuring themselves, she was sure they would've noticed it. And if they had, they no doubt would've run it off or, worse, done something to harm it. If she could keep them from noticing, she'd get a chance to find out what it was.

"Uh, guys?"

Their sharp gazes turned her way.

"Yeah?" asked Raine.

"How about waiting for me in the water? By the waterfall?" Did her voice sound seductive enough to keep their focus on her? "Unless you're too tired to have a little more fun?"

"Touching fun?" Pete was already heading toward the water.

"Oh, most definitely."

"Then meet us behind the waterfall. There's a break in the fall and a ledge in the back." Blue wasn't far behind Pete with Raine taking up the rear.

That sounded almost interesting enough to divert her from her first idea. "Great. I'll be there in a minute after I check out the shots I took."

"Yeah, let's have a look."

Her heart did a flip-flop as Pete diverted from his course. She darted her gaze to the creature to make sure it was still there then back to Pete. "No, no. I want to check them out on my own. You go on ahead with your brothers. See? They're already halfway there."

"Okay." He rushed to the pool, then waded in and dove under the water.

She waited a moment longer before moving swiftly toward the forest. When she was within a few feet of the creature, she paused, giving it time to realize that she meant it no harm. With luck, he wouldn't hurt her, either.

"Hey there."

She didn't know why she half-expected to get an answer. He had intelligence in his red eyes that made her think he might be more than an animal, but that was it. His mouth, more a muzzle, couldn't have formed words. At least not words she could understand.

She inched forward. He remained still, his focus on her and nothing else. Would he flee if she brought the camera up to her face? Not wanting to take the chance, she held it at chest level and did her best to aim it at him. Once she got closer, hopefully, he'd get more comfortable and she'd take a chance at getting a better shot.

"Don't be afraid. I won't hurt you."

His face scrunched up as it had the first time she'd seen him.

"You won't hurt me, will you, Scrunch?"

He didn't seem dangerous to her. Maybe the men had the creature all wrong. Or maybe she'd encountered a peaceful one of his kind. Either way, she'd take care, but she'd give him the benefit of the doubt, too.

A low sound rumbled out of him as his attention flicked to the water. She checked to make sure the men weren't coming. They must've already made it behind the fall.

"It's okay. They won't hurt you, either. See? They're gone."

Not that she didn't want them close enough to hear her if she called for help.

Scrunch hunkered down, leaning forward on long arms that seemed more human than animal. His knuckles brushed the ground much like an ape's would when it walked. He was hairless, his black skin as shiny as a fur coat, with his flesh stretched over a bone-thin frame. Small ears pressed flat against his head.

She clicked, taking a photo. The slits in his head that served as his nose quivered and a long, black tongue lashed over his thin upper lip.

She should run. Scream. Do something other than stand there and take a picture of the hideous thing. But she couldn't. He wouldn't hurt her. Now that she'd gotten closer, she knew it was true. But what was it? Part animal and part human? The Missing Link? She caught a movement below and dropped her gaze.

Oh, hell. I already saw enough of his cock the first time. She pulled her gaze away as fast as she could.

"That's it, Scrunch. Take it easy. But you better know that if you come at me with that thing, I'm going to run like hell. Which means the three big guys you saw will be on you like white on rice."

Scrunch tilted his head, reminding her of the way the men had tilted theirs in question. Was it a coincidence? Or did it mean more than that? She ignored the errant thought and decided Scrunch was comfortable enough for her to lift her camera to her face. Besides, she didn't want to take shots of just his dick.

Taking it slowly, she lifted the camera and centered the photo in the frame. Scrunch flicked out his tongue again, but remained where he was. She didn't waste any time, and took several pictures in succession.

But when he picked up a banana and held it out to her, she forgot all about what she was doing. She lowered the camera and frowned at him.

Did she dare accept his offer? Or was he drawing her closer so he could grab her?

She pushed down the clanging of alarms raging in her head. If she were smart, she'd back off while she could. But curiosity got the better of her.

Putting her camera beside her feet, she took the banana and started peeling it. Once peeled, she broke it into halves and handed one of the pieces to Scrunch. "I hate eating alone, too."

They chewed the banana, woman and creature regarding each

other with open interest. "See? You're not so scary."

"Callie, get away from it!"

Scrunch dropped the remainder of his fruit, let out a sound resembling a girl's screech, and disappeared into the woods. She whirled toward Pete's shout and saw the brothers charging through the pool then onto land. Without bothering to get dressed, they dashed past her in pursuit of Scrunch.

"No! Stop! Come back!"

When they kept running, breaking through the trees and underbrush, she did the only thing she could think to do. Drawing in a big breath, she let out a bloodcurdling scream.

Within a few seconds, Blue reappeared, bringing his brothers along with him. "Are there more of them?" He scanned the area around her, just as Pete and Raine did. "I don't see any."

"That's because you ran off the only one that was here."

The concern on his face morphed into irritation. "Then why the hell did you scream for us to come back?"

"I had to do something to get you guys to stop chasing that poor thing. He wasn't doing anything to harm me."

Blue opened his mouth to speak again then slammed it shut. Pete muttered a curse while Raine gave her a hard stare.

"You don't know what you're messing with, Callie."

"Then don't you think it's about time you tell me, Pete? The only thing I've heard is that he's dangerous and I should stay away from him."

"So why aren't you heeding our warning? And it's an *it*. Not a he."

"Whatever *he* is, he isn't dangerous. Not once did I feel threatened. Not when I saw him at the pit, and not here." She hadn't told them the total truth and had, in fact, been afraid of Scrunch. Or leery to say the least. But they didn't need to know that.

The men dressed, each glancing toward the forest. Blue stalked over to her and grabbed her arm.

"Hey! You're hurting me."

"I'm trying to save your pretty hide."

He pushed her to the rock and motioned for her to sit down. Although she wanted to refuse simply on the principle that she didn't like him ordering her around, she pushed herself onto the rock then crossed her arms. "Do tell."

"You were told that they were trouble and you didn't listen. Are you listening now?"

"Go ahead. Give it your best shot. But I know what I know."

"You don't know a damn thing."

Raine edged his brother away and urged him to calm down. Once Blue had done so, he confronted her. "Callie, you don't understand."

She softened a little and decided that maybe she should hear them out. If she really trusted them—and she did—then she had to give them the chance to say their piece. But why wouldn't they trust her when it came to Scrunch? "Fine. Then make me understand. What has he done to you?"

"I don't know that he's done anything, but his kind have." He settled on the rock beside her and she relaxed. As relaxed as she could get around any of the Deacon men. As soon as they got anywhere close to her, her body started to burn with need. She concentrated, determined not to let her wayward libido keep her from paying attention.

"They're called The Cursed."

"Tell me something I don't know." His sharp look kept her from going on. "Sorry."

"They're like us, but different. I know it's hard to believe, but the tales say that they were born to, uh, werewolves, but that they couldn't change right."

If he hadn't looked so serious, she would've laughed. "Werewolves? You're kidding me, right?"

"No, I'm not. Things are different inside The Hidden. We have things, beings here that myths and fairy tales are made of."

"I know this place is thought to be magical, but I didn't know I should take that literally." Her incredulousness, however, was getting harder to hang on to.

"Yeah, I know it's hard to believe, but have you ever seen anything like it, like him before?"

"No, but..." Her nerves leapt to life. Hadn't she had a similar thought? That he was the Missing Link? If what they said was true, then what was Scrunch really?

"From what we know, the children of werewolves will transform within a few weeks of being born. But those poor creatures we call The Cursed can't go through the change. Instead, their ancestors were born like that, caught in a partial transformation. They're stuck being half-werewolf and half-human."

"And you're saying Scrunch is one of these Cursed things?"

"Scrunch?" Blue gaped at her. "You named it?"

"Never mind that." Pete took her hand. "They're dangerous because they hate our people for being human and for having the lives we have. They're animals and unable to control themselves. They usually attack at night and against one or two of us while we're in the forest, but that's not always the case. The fact that your Scrunch is out right now and got that close to you proves it."

"Damn. Don't you start calling him that name. And sure as shit don't call it hers."

"Relax, Blue." Pete squeezed her hand. "Do you understand why we don't want you near him? We're afraid for your life."

"Do you really think he'd hurt me? That he might even kill me?"

"They've killed before. And if he scratches you, it could make you very ill. Possibly even kill you. We can't let that happen."

"But why would he? He didn't act like he hated me. In fact, I'd say he's trying to do the exact opposite. Like he's trying to make friends with me. Maybe these Cursed things are trying to change. Or maybe it's just him. Either way, I don't think he'd hurt me."

"Maybe he wouldn't, but we don't want to take that chance."

"Pete, come on."

He waved off Raine's objection. "You have to know one more thing. The Cursed want to mate with a human woman. They think that if they do, their children will have more human blood running in their veins. The more generations that mate with a human woman, the closer it brings their kind to becoming like us."

Her throat closed up. She didn't mind befriending Scrunch, but the idea of one of them taking her was unthinkable.

"Don't worry. We won't let them get to you."

She nodded, understanding as much as she could. It would take more time to get it to sink it. Still, she couldn't shake the impression that Scrunch would never do anything to her.

Pete brushed her hair away from her cheek. "Let's get back home, okay?"

She started to deny that the camp was her home, but didn't. A feeling of warmth washed over her. What would it be like to have a real home? And how amazing would it be to have a home like The Hidden with the Deacon men in her life? They'd stood up for her, protected her as no one had ever done. She'd let her guard down and, for once, she'd placed her trust in the right place and with the right men. Letting Pete help her, she slid off the rock and kept his hand as they walked back to camp.

* * * *

Callie strolled from one side of the campsite to the other. After what Pete had told her about The Cursed, she'd needed time to think and she'd asked the men to give her the rest of that day and the next. After all, what was the rush? According to them, she wasn't going anywhere.

Besides, wasn't anticipation part of the fun of a new relationship? With three luscious men wanting to take her into their bed, the anticipation was that much better.

What she hadn't counted on was finding so much to see around the camp that she ended up not thinking about Scrunch and the Deacons at all.

The people here are amazing. Strange, but amazing.

Maybe it was her surroundings, or Scrunch, or the way she'd gone wild with the Deacon men, but she was beginning to wonder if she'd lost her mind. Why else would she start imagining so many things? Like when she'd almost run into two women with odd silver eyes. Surprised, she'd come to a quick stop and was thrown by their exotic look. But the eyes weren't the most unusual thing about them. For a moment, too fast for her to be sure, she would've sworn she'd seen wings on their backs.

She'd stopped to gawk until Luke, the larger-than-life man, had swept by her. He'd mumbled a "Hey" in greeting and she'd answered. Then, turning around to give her a big grin, she'd seen his face. Fur covered most of his face. Stunned, she'd timidly pointed it out to him, but he'd acted unconcerned. Instead, he'd widened his huge grin, added a "Yup," and hurried on his way.

"I'm losing it big time."

"Losing what? I can help you find it. I'm very good at finding things."

"Oh, I didn't see you there." She regarded the boy in his late teens that had snuck up behind her. "No thanks. I didn't lose anything."

"So you aren't trying to find something?" His dark eyes flashed in his wide face as the breeze blew his black hair around.

"No. Just my mind."

He tilted his head to the side, reminding her of her men…and a little of Scrunch. "You're with the Deacon brothers." He leaned closer.

Did he just sniff me?

"Yeah. I guess you could say I am. Well, it was nice talking to you." She pivoted on her heel, intending to give him a polite brush-off, but he fell into step at her side.

"They're great guys."

"Uh-huh."

"Yeah. I've known them all my life."

"That's great." *Why is he tagging along with me?*

"A woman couldn't do better than to have them as her mates."

She swung toward him, her focus momentarily misdirected by the sight of a rabbit standing among the bushes. Wasn't there a little girl there just a second ago?

"So? Are you?"

She watched the bunny hop off. "Am I what?"

"Are you going to be their mate? Man, if I could have even one of them as my mate, I'd be the happiest man in the world."

Oh. So he's gay. The poor kid must have it rough knowing the objects of his affection are heterosexual. Or could they be bi? I should ask. But then again, why should I since I'm not planning on sticking around?

"I don't know." Now why hadn't she said no?

She cared for them and was entranced by The Hidden. But did that mean she'd stay? If she didn't, would she ever see them again?

"Is it because they're different from you?"

Pot? Kettle calling.

"How do you mean 'different'?"

The color in his face washed away. "I can't say."

She narrowed her eyes and tilted her head at him in imitation of his gesture. "Yes, you can. Talk."

"That's not for me to say. But please remember one thing."

His obvious concern was mysterious. "What's that?"

"Remember that no matter what's underneath, they're still the same men you're falling in love with."

Underneath what? "Wait a second. Who says I'm falling in love with them?" That was impossible, and yet, her heart claimed that it might be true.

"They're waiting for you, you know."

This kid is full of surprises.

She craned her neck toward their tent.

"Not in the tent." He pointed toward one of the cabins built into the side of a hill. "There."

"And you know this because…?"

"Because they sent me to find you." He winked at her and hurried off, leaving her with more questions than answers.

They're waiting for me.

She didn't want it to, not until she'd sorted out her feelings, but she couldn't deny that her pulse picked up speed. She hadn't seen them since yesterday and now she realized how much she'd missed them.

Trying not to break into a run, she strode toward the cabin. Once there, she lifted her hand to knock on the door, then grabbed the door handle, and pushed the door open.

The sun was setting at her back and casting her shadow into the candlelit room. She inhaled the aroma of fresh flowers that filled the big open area and took in her surroundings. The men were nowhere in sight, but red rose petals were strewn along the floor, leading into the big open living area toward one of three doors at the back of the home.

She turned to close the door behind her and saw that several people had stopped to watch her. As soon as they saw that she'd noticed them, they moved on, hurrying about their business.

Damn it all. Is everyone in on this?

She shut the door then turned to face the trail of petals. *Here goes nothing. Or everything.*

She'd made it to the end of the hallway before the thought hit her. Why did she have the feeling that once, hell, *if,* she entered the room, that her life would change forever? And if it did, would it change for the better or for the worse?

Go inside.

Listening to her inner voice, she pushed the door wide. The

Deacon men, all naked, were in various positions with Blue reclining on a huge bed and Pete tucked into a leather easy chair. Raine leaned against the wall, adopting a suave position and holding a rose in his mouth. White candles of various sizes cast pretty shadows on the walls and flowers filled the room.

She laughed, loving the mix of humor and romance. "I hear you're looking for me."

Raine spit the flower out of his mouth. "Damn straight we are." He cupped his hands over his flaccid cock. "It's about time you showed up. We were getting cold waiting for you."

"Really? Because from what I can tell it's hellaciously warm in here."

"Get over here and I'll show you what warm is." Pete patted his lap.

"Never mind him." Raine strode over to her and presented the flower to her. "Let me show you how hot it can get."

Feeling like a princess in a storybook, she took the rose and held it to her nose. But she wasn't interested in its fragrance as much as she wanted a moment longer to stare at the men.

Maybe I got lucky when the buck chased me into the pit.

Raine placed his hands on her hips and tugged her to him. His hands slid to the rise of her butt cheeks as he bent over and placed a kiss on her neck. "Tell us you want to be with us, all of us, as much as we want you."

Her mind as well as her body worked on impulse. "Yes. I do."

"Bring her to the bed, Raine."

Raine pulled away and stared. His blue eyes sparkled with his lust. Flecks of amber glowed in them, and without giving it real thought, she wondered what that meant. She'd seen the amber bits in Blue's eyes as well and had assumed it was a family trait. But then how did that explain the color in Pete's?

Raine took her hand and brought her to the bed. His cock pressed against her leg as he stood to the side while Pete moved to her other side. Pete's shaft was as ready as his brother's. Her gaze drifted to Blue, who still lay on the bed and slid his hand down to take his equally impressive cock.

Taking their time, they took hold of the hem of her dress and slinked it up her legs. They stopped at her waist, as though they'd taken a silent cue from each other, making the dress drape in the front and back.

"I'm so glad the women don't bother themselves with panties or thongs."

"Oh, I don't know, Pete. I like the way a woman looks in one of those lacy panties, especially when it shows part of her butt."

Was Raine complaining? Should she have put on the panties she'd wore the day they'd met? She'd chosen the custom of going without because she'd loved how free it made her feel.

Raine eased his palm over to her mons. "Then again, this is terrific, too."

Pete did the same and she thought their fingers might meet. Instead, Raine brought his hand back, then around the curve of her hip to grab her butt cheek.

Heat swirled inside her and even the air in the room around her grew warm and heavy. Desire surrounded them. "Pete?"

"Shh. Don't talk. We can talk later."

She jumped as Pete pushed a finger between her folds. Swallowing, she tried to stand still, tried to take it in stride, and failed.

His finger found her clit as it started throbbing. She was wet, knowing that it spread over his finger and maybe onto his palm. Her breathing quickened and she reached out to take his cock. Now it was his turn to jump.

She turned her focus to Pete and him alone and began stroking. Two could play at the teasing game.

He sped his movements up. She did the same, but having to match his quick, short strokes with her long ones put her at a disadvantage in winning this impromptu competition. She smiled and pumped her hand harder.

Raine took hold of both sides of her dress and tugged it over her head, making her turn Pete's cock loose as he did. She took it again fast enough, but didn't count on Raine moving behind her. The combination of both brothers' hands, then their mouths—*ooh! tongues!*—on her ratcheted up the sensations. Her body tightened even as she loosened up, ready to welcome them inside her in whatever way they wanted.

Raine squeezed her butt cheeks and snaked his tongue along her shoulder. She reached behind her, trying to take hold of his cock, but he pushed it against her butt crack and she couldn't get to it. Groaning, she brought her hand up and grabbed for his hair.

Pete's rubbing on her clit intensified and her panting grew louder. Her legs grew weak and she wasn't sure she could stand up much longer. Yet she knew Raine and Pete wouldn't let her fall. Whimpering, she grabbed Pete's hand and pulled it away.

"What's the matter? I thought you liked what I was doing."

She caught her breath and smiled. "I did. But don't you think"— she lifted his hand and brought his finger to her mouth—"you'd like to get a taste of me?" She sucked her juices off then pulled his finger out with a satisfying *pop.*

A glance at Blue found him pumping his cock even faster. His eyes were cloudy with need.

"I like the way you think." Pete traveled his tongue down her shoulder, along the curve of her breast to make his way over her waist and along the side of her hip. With one more look her way, he scooted in front of her to rest between her legs, and pressed his mouth to her pussy.

Her knees gave way, and if Raine hadn't held her up from behind, she would've gone down. She clutched Pete's hair as he parted her pussy lips and lashed his tongue over her clit.

"Yeah. Please. More."

Raine, still supporting her with one arm under hers, fondled her butt. "Damn, girl, but you've got a great ass."

She craned her neck to see him. "If you really think so, then spank it." She'd never engaged in any sexual spanking, but with the Deacon brothers, she really wanted to.

Raine's growl vibrated through his chest and into her back. "My pleasure." He whacked her butt then spanked her a second time.

She yelped, and the split second of pain along with the lingering aftereffects gave her a rush of adrenaline and pure joy. "Do it again."

He did, spanking her harder. Pete sucked on her clit, driving a small orgasm out of her, and wrapped his hands around her legs to hold her up.

"Lean over, Callie."

She did, following Raine's directions to bend over and put her palms flat on Pete's back. Pete crawled in between her legs and drove two fingers into her pussy. His tongue tormented her clit.

"Oh. My. God," she breathed. They knew how to use their hands, how to make her body tingle under their touches.

"That-a-girl. Now hang on. You're going to love this."

Another hit came to her right cheek and she could feel her flesh ripple from the strike. Raine pushed her lower and spanked her again for a second and third time.

"I'm going to fuck your ass now."

She tossed her hair over her shoulder and glanced at Raine. "Do it. But don't stop spanking me."

He grinned and whacked her again. The blow was so hard that she wobbled on her feet and had to brace herself to keep her from tumbling over Pete.

Raine eased his cock against her dark hole. "Shit, you're tight. Blue, toss me some lube."

Blue grumbled something she couldn't make out. The words, if they were indeed words, were jumbled and sounded almost nonhuman. But she couldn't see anything different about him as he leaned over to grab a small tube from the nightstand.

Damn, his cock is huge. She swallowed, hard.

"Here you go."

A few seconds later and a cool substance slid down her crack. Raine followed it with his hand and then pushed his lubricated fingers into her butt hole.

She trembled in anticipation and alarm. No man had ever taken her from behind, but she was more than ready to find out how it felt. "Go on, Raine."

"Easy, girl. We don't want you to get hurt."

"Thanks, but I need you to do this. Now." She trembled, nervous, but ready.

Raine's chuckle gave her the reassurance that it would be all right. Easing his cock inside slowly, he pushed in, and her anus muscles made way.

She hadn't known what it would be like, but she hadn't expected it to feel so damn good. She moaned and lowered her head, letting the brief moment of pain wash away to be replaced by sheer need. Pete's eyes were closed, his fingers pumping into her pussy as he sucked and licked on her clit.

Her moans grew louder as she watched one brother eat her and felt the other pull his cock out of her ass then thrust back inside with a powerful shove. He grunted his pleasure then shoved inside her again.

A storm of emotions mixed with thundering sexual sensations. Her body was their instrument and they were playing her like the masterful musicians they were.

"Guys, you'd better get her into bed before I knock you both out of the way and take her. I'm the one who hasn't had her yet."

"Hang. On," panted Raine as he clutched her hips and drove into her harder. His balls flapped against her.

Pete shoved another finger inside her pussy and latched onto her clit again. Using his teeth to hold her, he flicked his tongue over her pulsating clit. Another larger climax ripped out of her and she closed her eyes to savor the entire experience.

Her body shivered as wave after wave rolled outward from her core. She held on, gritting her teeth as Raine's motions sped up. His fingers dug into her skin and a low rumble flowed out of him. The rumble transformed into a low growl and then into a sound resembling a howl as he slammed into her one last time. He pulled out of her and shot his cum over her lower back.

Pete pulled away and got to his feet to steady her. Raine's grunts grew softer as his release warmed her skin.

"Hang on. I'll get something to clean you off."

"Here." Blue jerked a pillow out of its case and tossed it to his brother. "And hurry the hell up."

She stayed bent over, waiting for Raine to clean her. Pete, in a crouch in front of her, took her face and put his mouth to hers.

The taste of her own juices along with the flavor of his mouth swept in with his tongue. She loved it and sucked on him, determined to get even more of it. But he didn't give her more. Instead, he broke the kiss then stood to bring her into his arms.

As Raine stumbled away, Pete looked deep into her eyes. "So you like it a little rough?"

"If you're asking if I liked the spanking, then yes, I did." Her butt cheeks still felt sensitive. "Do you?" Before he could answer, she swatted him on the butt cheek.

"Hey! We'll do the spanking here. Remember that." He lifted her under the arms and tossed her on top of the bed. She squealed then tried to scramble away, but Pete snagged her by the ankle and dragged her back. He positioned her with her butt hanging halfway over the bed then pushed her legs apart.

Giving her a whack on the side of the leg, he took hold of her again and shoved his cock inside her. She squirmed, halfheartedly trying to get away, when Blue grabbed her wrists and held them over her head. His oozing cock was only a few inches from her face.

"Suck on me."

She wanted to play, to tease. "No. I'm not your captive."

An eyebrow arched. "Maybe not, but you're our woman and I told you to suck on me." To emphasize his words, he pinched her nipple.

She cried out and fought to get free. Sort of. "No."

Another tweak of her nipple came along with a spank on the side of her butt cheek from Pete. He rammed into her again, then again before adding another spank to the other hip.

"Callie."

She couldn't help but look at Blue. "Yes?"

"You're ours. Not as a captive, but as our woman. And we're yours. Know that." He gritted his teeth and the muscles in his jaw danced. "Now suck me."

His words broke away more pieces of the barrier she'd built around her heart throughout her childhood and into adulthood. They'd claimed her, even commanding her at times, but she'd never felt weak, used, or betrayed by them. Instead, the more they wanted from her, the more she wanted to give to them. And she knew they'd give all of themselves to her in return.

She quit playing the game and opened her mouth. He turned her hands loose and she wrapped her hand around his cock. He was musky smelling, soft and hard at the same time, and huge, filling her mouth. Taking hold of her hair, he helped her to move her head back and forth, drawing him in and then releasing him.

"Play with yourself."

She reached down as Blue commanded and rubbed her wet pussy. Pete's cock bumped against her fingers, adding more to her already growing need.

The Deacon brothers were the hottest men she'd ever seen and she was having all three of them. If her mouth wasn't so busy, she'd shout for joy.

Blue's grip on her hair hurt, but in a way that only helped to tantalize her more. He softened his hold on her breast, no longer pinching it and, instead, fondled it as he rubbed his palm back and forth over her skin.

Pete's thrusts grew faster, harder. His gaze was on her pussy, watching her torture herself. With another slap on her butt, he pushed in one last time then pulled out, shouting his release.

"It's about time I get you."

Blue yanked on her hair, eliciting a yelp from her, then clutched her arms and pulled her along with him as he fell backward. She landed on top of him, and without warning, he rammed his cock inside her pussy.

She cried out as he sunk deep inside her. He covered her breasts with his hands and she did the same, trying to stay on the thrusting man. His expression was intense, his gaze locked to hers as he worked his hips upward, driving his cock deep within her pussy.

Pete crawled onto the bed beside her and whacked her on the butt cheek again. The pain from that combined with the sensation of Blue's cock straining against her pussy walls. She cried out, then shouted again when Pete grabbed her hair and pulled her head back. He kissed her hard and slapped her butt again.

They treated her roughly, but she loved it. Her body hurt and ached in all the right places. Sweat formed along her brow as she matched each man's fervor by kissing Pete harder and grinding her body against Blue's.

When Pete let go of her hair, he leaned over and nibbled along her shoulder. His hands gripped her butt cheeks, adding a slap or two. She looked at Blue and found him staring at her again, but his expression was one that she hadn't seen before. One that she almost didn't recognize.

She'd swear he was looking at her with love.

He spoke as if he'd heard her thoughts. "We care about you, Callie. More than you realize. But you will. You will."

She froze, then at the urging of another slap from Pete, rocked against him. They cared for her. Yet what that meant was unclear. Although different words started to form in her mouth, she said, "I care for you, too."

Blue's expression clouded then he shoved into her again. He held on to her as he brought his upper torso up and took her face in his hands. Her breath hitched in her throat as she waited to hear what he'd tell her.

"No, you're not getting it." His amber-filled eyes blazed. "I, we, love you."

Something deep inside her recognized the truth and burst to life. A wildness threatened to overtake her, and for a split second, she saw the world through a flash of amber. Lust, pure and simple, surged wild and an inner voice, an ache-filled howl, echoed in her ears.

With one last thrust, he closed his eyes and pulled her to him, flattening her breasts to his massive chest. Much like Raine had done, he growled and, as his climax took him, roared his release.

She answered with her own climax, the biggest and strongest of orgasms spilling out of her to flood over his cock. Her body shook as she lost rational thought and gave in to the primal reactions taking control of her body. Rush after rush whipped through her, easing a little with each subsequent roll until her body lost its strength and she fell against Blue.

He pulled her along with him to lie on the bed. Pete and Raine joined them with Pete settling at her other side and Raine at her feet.

"Did you hear what I said?" Blue lay on his back, his attention on the ceiling, and didn't look her way.

Was he afraid, too? If so, she'd understand. She was fearful of what she'd see in his eyes.

What did he want her to say? That she loved them back? She'd have to tell them that she didn't and she tried. How could she say those words when she wasn't sure she wanted to stay? But the words wouldn't come. "I did."

Pete took her arm, making her look at him. "It's true, but you don't have to say anything right now. We realize it's a lot to take in. But understand this. That thing you've felt between us—" He narrowed his eyes. "And yes, we know you've felt it because we have. That thing is a connection between us. It's an irresistible pull from men like us and the woman we intend to take as our mate."

She knew what he was talking about, although she hadn't known what to call it. Love at first sight? Supercharged lust? Whatever it was, could she trust it? Was it even possible for such a thing to exist? Yet she knew the truth in her gut.

"I-I don't understand." She pressed her palm to her forehead. "None of what you're saying makes any sense. I barely know you. Any of you."

Why was she denying it? Hadn't she already known before she'd walked into the room?

Blue turned to her at last. "Yes, you do. You know us in your heart where it counts. Knowing the stupid things about us like what our favorite food is, or getting used to our lifestyle doesn't matter." He fisted his hand against his chest. "The only thing that matters is what's in here."

She half expected his brothers to make fun of him for sounding so romantic, but they didn't. Instead, she saw his words reflected on their faces.

"Pete's right. Don't say anything yet. Just think about us. Think about how you've felt since the first moment you met us." He rolled away from her. "Come on, guys. Give her a little space to think. Callie, we're staying here for the night. All of us."

Raine walked around the room, putting out the candles while his brothers settled around her. He joined them, not touching her and not speaking.

Darkness slowly overtook the room. She stared into the night as the moon filtered in through the sheer curtains. Within a few minutes, she heard the sounds of the men sleeping.

They love me. Holy shit.

A smile formed on her face as sleep took her away.

* * * *

Callie stretched and crawled out from between the three men who had suddenly become so important to her. She'd heard of men and women falling in love in a week or so, but she'd never thought she'd fall for not only one, but three men in the space of less than a weekend.

What am I going to do?

They hadn't *invited* her to stay. Instead they'd told her she couldn't leave, which wasn't the same thing. Yet, if they did ask, what would her answer be? The peaceful campsite below was dotted with campfires. Couples as well as groups of people strolled around the area or sat basking in the light of the fires. A young girl's giggles floated on the air, followed by the deeper tones of a young man. Fireflies made twinkling lights against the darkness and she sighed, pressing her hands to the windowpane.

Surely it couldn't be this idyllic all the time? Every place, no matter how beautiful, had its darker side. Were the creatures like Scrunch the underbelly of The Hidden? But what if Scrunch was indicative of a change? What if he was a new breed of his kind? A new, kinder, gentler side of them? What if his reaching out to her was a first step toward reconciliation between the people of The Hidden and The Cursed?

Sheesh! What next, Callie? Running for office?

Red eyes blinked at her from a bush near the cabin but far enough away and uphill from the others that she doubted they noticed it. She glanced back at the sleeping men, making not-so-soft snoring sounds, then squinted into the darkness.

Was it Scrunch? Or another one of The Cursed?

She had to find out. Why would Scrunch risk coming so close unless he needed her? Although she wasn't sure he'd see her or even understand, she gave him a little wave to say she'd come outside.

Gathering her dress and shoes, she slipped out of the bedroom and padded her way to the front door. Throwing her dress over her head as she pushed her feet into the moccasins, she turned the knob and eased into the night. She paused and listened for any sign that she'd awakened the men. Hearing nothing, she hurried down the steps then angled to the left. She came to the bushes where she'd seen the red eyes, but couldn't find them again. Had it all been an illusion?

"Scrunch? Is that you?"

The men would turn her over their knees and spank her for real if they caught her. She tried again, raising her voice a little. "Scrunch?"

He poked his head out of the bush, then pushed his hand through. She almost laughed when she saw the banana in his hand.

"Are you bringing me a midnight snack?"

He peeled the banana, doing it in much the same way she'd done. Breaking it in half, he handed her a piece. She took it and chomped off a large bite. "Yeah, it's really tasty."

She covered her mouth as she spoke with it full of the fruit and checked to make sure no one had heard her. "But this isn't worth getting your butt kicked for. Is there something else? What do you want?"

He pulled away, disappearing into the dark recesses and making her take the chance to lean toward him. His claw-like hand wrapped around her arm and she let out a quick squeal that was cut off when he yanked her through the branches. The rough ride scratched her arms and face, but he soon turned her loose once she was on the other side.

"You could've asked me, you know." She inspected her skin. "Thanks for nothing."

He cocked his head to the side and made a noise that sounded like a mix of a growl and a groan. Then, after giving her arm a quick tug, he spun around and ambled off, his knuckles scraping the ground.

She took off after him, knowing she was putting herself at risk. But she couldn't not go. She had to find what he wanted. Unlike what they'd told her, Scrunch was more intelligent than a mere animal.

But keeping up with him was not easy. "Wait up. I can't move as fast as you."

Every time she tried to get him to slow down, Scrunch whirled around in a circle, gave her a quick glance, then took off again. She tried to move at a quicker rate, but running at night without a light had almost sent her falling face-first into the dirt twice already. If the moon hadn't been out and the sky cloudless, she wouldn't have had a chance of catching up with him.

"Come on. Don't go so fast, for Pete's sake."

Pete's going to have my head. If he doesn't kill me first. Figuratively speaking, I hope.

Scrunch spun around again then let out a shriek and took off.

"No! Scrunch, hold up!" Heedless of the possibility of falling, she took off running. She didn't know where they were or where he was leading her, but she wasn't about to give up.

Someone took hold of her shoulder and wrenched her around. Her hair flew across her face and she whipped it away, fearing what she might see.

"What the hell do you think you're doing?" Pete was angry. Very angry. Blue and Raine raced by her, chasing Scrunch.

"Let me go!"

But he held her, his fingers digging into her skin. "Not on your life. Hell, not *for* your life."

"I told you to let me go!"

He shook his vigorously. "No."

She'd have to try a different method. Pushing her mouth into a pout, she batted her eyelids and attempted to muster up a few tears. "But, Pete, you're hurting me."

He sucked in a quick breath and turned her loose. "Shit, Callie, I never meant to—"

She took off running before he'd ended his sentence, calling over her shoulder. "I can't believe you bought that."

The screech that tore the night apart sent her speeding ahead. It was as if an inner ability she hadn't known she possessed had opened up, and without her understanding why, had given her a burst of high energy. The world shifted, the dark grays and blacks of the night tinging with an amber color. Her heart pounded, but not from exertion. Instead, it came from the thrill of running under the moon.

She lowered her head and, hearing Pete's footsteps behind her, barreled ahead. If Raine hadn't caught her, scooping her up into his arms, she would've fallen into the same hole where Scrunch sat crouched in a corner.

Instead of struggling, she brought her gaze to Raine's. An internal explosion broke through her, awakening a new inner voice, and she heard the howl of a wolf deep inside her. She flattened her hand against his hard chest and felt his heart beating in unison to hers.

She inhaled, drawing in the scent of the other two men. Was their aroma stronger from their run? Yet none of them were sweating.

A quieter, shorter version of the screech she'd heard before came from the pit. "Put me down, Raine."

He checked with his brothers, who both had the sense enough not to object. Placing her on her feet, he took her wrist before she could move to the side of the hole. "He's okay."

"He damn well better be." She yanked her hand away. She wasn't angry so much as worried for Scrunch. Careful not to lean too far, she peered over the edge and gave the whimpering Scrunch a comforting smile.

"It's okay, buddy. We'll get you out."

"You have got to be out of your mind." Blue paced to her side. "First, you get out of bed and leave us to go chasing after this thing and now you want us to help him? What next? Should we have a party and invite all The Cursed?"

"Take it easy, bro," warned Pete.

"Are you fucking crazy, too? We have been taking it easy. Too easy. And look where that's gotten us. Standing over a damn trap in the middle of the night while our mate plays Jane to his Tarzan."

Had she heard him right? "What'd you say?"

"You heard me. There's nothing wrong with your ears."

"Or her eyes." Raine jutted out his chin at her.

"What are you talking about? What about my eyes?"

"Let's stick to the subject at hand."

She prodded him in the middle of his chest. As soon as she touched him, a lot of her irritation went away and was replaced by a lust that almost knocked her off her feet. But that was for later. "I asked you what you said. Did you call me your mate?"

"Yeah, I did. We told you as much earlier."

But had they used that word?

Scrunch let out another wail, interrupting their conversation. He scampered to the other side of the hole. She'd have to continue the conversation about being their mate later. After she got Scrunch out of the pit.

"We're going to get him out. I know what it feels like to be stuck in a hole." She didn't care what they said. They'd help her get him out. One way or another, she'd make them see it her way.

"No. We're not." Blue crossed his arms over his chest and glared at her. "As far as I'm concerned, he can stay down there until he rots."

She dropped her jaw in horror. "That is so not the nice guy I thought you were. Is that how all of you feel? Can you really leave the poor little thing to die?"

Pete shifted on his feet. "Blue, maybe we should get him out."

"And risk getting bitten?" Blue's eyes flashed a strange amber color. "No way."

"How bad can he bite you?" She didn't mention that Scrunch had very long fangs, but he'd never tried to hurt her. "Besides, you're bigger and stronger. Can't the three of you subdue him?"

"It's not that." Raine ran a hand through his hair. "Their bites are deadly to us. Just one bite and we could die."

She couldn't believe it. "Of all the things you should've told me, don't you think that should've been one of them?"

But that didn't lessen her resolve to help Scrunch. "Okay. So that just means we have to take even more care getting him out. For his sake as well as ours."

"I'm sorry, Callie, Blue's right."

Yet instead of fighting with Pete, she turned and got closer to the edge. "If you guys won't help him, then maybe you'll help me."

"What does that mean?"

She shot Blue a watch-and-see look then turned and jumped into the pit.

Chapter Seven

"What the hell are you doing now?" Pete scowled at her then backed up. Anger and fear swirled inside him, making a heady mix of emotions that threatened to bring out his wolf whether he wanted to shift or not.

Maybe he could've stopped her if he'd had any idea of what she was about to do. But she'd leapt over the edge before he could react.

"I'm not going to let you guys leave him here to die. If you do, then you're letting me die, too."

Blue cursed a blue streak and stalked away from the pit. Pete could see Raine trying to think of something to say, but what could that be? He strode back to the pit. "You're out of your mind. We told you. It's dangerous."

"Maybe some of the others of his kind are, but not Scrunch." She drew closer to the thing, adding another painful twist to Pete's gut.

"Callie, be reasonable. What do you expect us to do?"

"I expect you to treat him with the same respect you treat everything and everyone else." She tossed her hair back over her shoulders. "I expect you to help him."

"He's one of *them*," added Raine as though that would sway her.

"Tell me, Raine, what if it was something else down here? Like maybe a deer or a wolf? Would you leave it to starve to death?"

"That's not the same thing. Deer and wolves aren't our sworn enemies."

"So you'd help them? And who says The Cursed are your enemies? So far, I haven't seen them do anything to you."

Pete held up his hand to his brother. "You haven't been around long enough to know. They've attacked our people, even killed them. What else would you call them except enemies?"

She turned to Scrunch and Pete hoped she was starting to see the creature through clear eyes. But his hope died when she faced him again. Her clenched jaw told him that her determination had grown even stronger.

"What if they want a truce? What if it's time for peace?"

"Shit. Our mate is fucking delusional," muttered Blue.

Pete shot Blue a stern warning to keep him quiet. "That's not the case."

"You don't know that." She crossed her arms. "What if Scrunch trying to contact me is a first step? What if he's trying to connect with me? With everyone?"

Blue scowled. "You're a dreamer if ever I heard one."

"But what if she's right?" Pete could feel the wrath of Blue's anger as he turned on him. "Take it easy, bro. I'm only asking. After all, they haven't done much to bother us lately."

"That's because they don't have Burac to lead them." Blue stalked to the other side of the hole. "Trust me. They'll strike again."

Blue was probably right. But if so, why was Scrunch trying to contact Callie? If he'd wanted, he could've easily taken her.

"We're wasting time, guys. Prove that you care about me. What's it going to be? Are you going to help us or not?"

"Kill it."

Pete pivoted in sync with his brothers to find Wesley, one of the many werewolves in The Hidden, striding toward the pit along with two other werewolves.

"How'd you know we were here?"

"Tina saw Callie and that thing and asked us to see what was going on." He peered at Callie. "Has it bitten her?"

Pete's mouth was open, ready to say anything except the truth when Callie offered it up instead.

"He hasn't and he's not going to. He's my...friend." She darted her gaze away only to bring it back. "And why are you people running around butt-naked?"

Wesley's black eyes filled with amber. "She's kidding, right? Or is she off in the head?" He made a circling motion in the air next to his head, the universal sign for mental illness.

"She's neither one. She and Scrunch are...okay with each other." Pete planted his feet apart, ready for their reaction.

"Are you saying she's made friends with it?"

Mikea, Wesley's co-mate with Shira, snorted. "You can't make friends with those things. What are we waiting for? The Cursed made the pits to catch animals and even some of us. It's only right that one of them dies there."

"I agree. Let's get it." Shira, a small, yet fierce werewolf, snarled, bringing out her fangs as she started shifting.

"Our mate's right." Wesley followed her, the sound of his bones breaking and reforming making an accompaniment to the noise Shira's bones made.

Mikea growled and shifted his attention from Pete to a horrified-looking Callie. "You haven't told her yet, have you? I'm sorry about jumping the gun, guys, but my mates are right. We're taking that thing out of this world and sending it straight to hell."

Less than a minute later, the three had shifted into their werewolf bodies. They split up, each pacing to a side of the pit.

"Oh, my God."

Pete hated to see the fear on her face. What The Cursed hadn't done, their friends had. They'd terrified their mate.

She backed up as Scrunch snarled, baring his fangs, his red eyes hooked on the wolves above. "Guys, run while you can. Get away."

Her eyes grew as realization hit her. "They're like the ones that surrounded me in the other hole. Holy shit, they're werewolves. Please run, Pete!"

"This wasn't the way she was supposed to find out." Blue slid beside him.

"No, but it's the way she did and we have to deal with it. After we decide if we're going to let Wesley and his mates take the thing."

Callie, recognition showing on her face as she began to understand, begged them. "Please, don't let them hurt him."

He'd do anything for her, but could he do this? He glanced up to find Wesley hunkering down, ready to pounce.

Yes, I can.

The world shifted and took on an amber hue. The familiar pain rushed through his body as he changed. His inner wolf howled with relief mixed with exhilaration as he transformed then crooked his head to stare at his brothers.

Blue grumbled another curse then shifted, too. But Raine stood fast, shaking his head. "She doesn't understand about them. Maybe this is the way to make her get it."

Callie whirled and grabbed Scrunch's arm. Together, they huddled against the dirt wall, trying to get into a protective position. Not that it would help. Wesley and his mates would tear them apart with one swipe of their claws, then take their lives with a crunch of their massive jaws on their necks.

But Pete wasn't about to let that happen. Snarling, he rushed at Mikea. Hurling his body at his friend, he knocked the wolf over. They rolled several yards before each of them got to their feet.

Mikea's eyes burned with anger. Although he didn't have to say anything, Pete knew his friend felt betrayed. No one had ever chosen one of The Cursed over their own.

Snarls and growls erupted behind them, telling him that Blue had joined in the fight. But he couldn't take a chance to see. Instead, he had to watch for Mikea's next move. If he didn't, he'd leave himself open for attack.

Mikea jumped at him, his jaws open to sink into Pete's flesh. Pete didn't want to hurt his friend, but he couldn't allow Mikea to harm Callie even if it meant protecting one of The Cursed. He tried to duck, but Mikea struck him in the side, knocking him down.

Desperation swamped him as the big wolf pounced on top. Fighting from the bottom was never a good thing, but he bit and clawed at the wolf's underbelly until, at last, Mikea jumped off. He scrambled to his feet, coming up a foot from his friend's face.

"Callie, now!"

Raine's voice proved he was still in his human form, leaving him vulnerable to the wolves' attacks. Had he stayed that way to help her out of the hole? He wanted to see, but couldn't take his eyes from his opponent.

Mikea gazed past Pete and a howl ripped from his throat. He started to get around Pete, but he stopped him, using his body as a wall. He'd give Raine and Callie the time they needed.

"Shit! Shit!"

Raine's curses didn't make him feel any better. *Come on, bro, get it done.*

Mikea backed up, snarling, his focus clearly on what Raine and Callie were doing. With Mikea far enough away, Pete dared to look.

Blue was playing guard against the two other werewolves while Raine held Callie close to him. Scrunch crouched at the edge of the forest, his red eyes blazing, then, with a low growl, he scurried into the trees.

Mikea and the others reverted to their human forms. Pete and Blue did the same after getting closer to Raine and Callie.

"You chose that thing over your own kind." Mikea spit out the accusation.

"You gave us no choice. We chose the safety of our mate. If you'd tried to hurt it, then she would've tried to defend it." He doubted his argument would change their minds.

Wesley shook his head, but it was the way he regarded them, his face a mask of disdain, that hurt the most. "The Council will hear about this."

Blue stood tall next to him with a trickle of blood running down his chest. "We don't doubt it. And when they call for us, we'll come."

Shira narrowed her eyes at Callie. "I don't understand how any woman could do this to her mates. You brought shame to yourself as well as to your men."

Pete was proud of Callie as she held her head high and didn't cower under Shira's criticism. He could smell the fear wafting off her body, but she wouldn't buckle under. "That's not how I see it. I didn't want anyone hurt. Not Scrunch, not us, and not you."

"Scrunch? You gave it a name? It's a fucking animal."

Wesley spat on the ground at Pete's feet, but Pete ignored the disrespectful gesture. He couldn't blame his friend for being upset. If Callie hadn't gotten involved, he would've stepped aside and let Wesley and his mates kill Scrunch.

Aw, hell. She's got me calling him by his name.

Callie's curt laugh surprised him. "He's an animal? You're werewolves." She clutched at Raine's arm. "Every last one of you." Her accusatory eyes landed first on Blue, then him.

"Callie, we meant to tell you." Blue blew out a breath. "Just not this way."

She tightened her grip on Raine. "I can't believe it. They're werewolves."

Pete waited, knowing that his brother couldn't keep the truth about himself quiet any longer. Raine put his hand on top of hers. "Callie, please don't be frightened. None of us would ever hurt you. Not them, or Pete, or Blue. And not me, either."

She lifted her gaze to Raine's. "Oh, my God." Turning him loose, she backed away. "You're a werewolf, too?"

Rained nodded, his body slumping against her obvious alarm. "Yes."

"Fuck this. Let's go. We have to tell Tina and the others." Casting one last glare at them, Wesley motioned for Shira and Mikea to follow him. They turned on their heels and stalked into the darkness of the woods.

Pete watched them in silence even after he couldn't see them any longer. But he wanted to delay the moment he turned to face Callie. Would he still see fear in her eyes? When he did confront her, he found she'd put more space between them.

"Thank you so much." Callie clasped her hands in front of them. "I don't know what I would've done if you hadn't been there."

Relief swamped him, but it was gone with her next words.

"But I can't...I mean, you're werewolves." She backed up another foot. "I can't believe it."

Pete shot a warning look at his brothers. After seeing her eyes change, they knew that she had to be part werewolf. But now was not the time to tell her. She already had too much to deal with.

"Callie, please. You have to know we'd never do anything to hurt you. If we'd wanted to, we could have attacked you a thousand times before now." Pete eased closer. He didn't want to, but if they had to tie her up and drag her back to camp to keep her from running off into the woods, then he'd do it.

She stood her ground, glancing at the woods with longing. "Take me back to the camp."

"Sure, Callie."

"But nothing else is going to happen." She scanned them one by one, then eased around them, keeping her distance. "No more physical stuff until I can get my mind wrapped around this. I still can't...It's impossible."

"If that's what you want." He didn't have to check with Blue and Raine. He knew they'd do whatever it took to get her back safe and sound.

"Good. But if I see one tiny bit of amber in your eyes or I think your teeth are getting longer, then I'm gone." She stopped, and searched the bushes, then waved them ahead of her. "I don't know which way to go. You first."

He relaxed a little. At least she was coming with them. They headed back to camp and had gotten halfway there when the first question came.

"Are there more werewolves here? In the camp?"

He answered without looking back. "Yes. And more than werewolves. There are werebears, werecats, and other supernatural beings."

She remained quiet for several minutes before asking, "Other supernatural beings? Like vampires?"

"We've had a few of them from time to time. But they're not much on joining with others, especially were-people like us. We do have fairies, elves, trolls, and others."

She let out a ragged sigh. "No wonder a lot of them seemed strange with long teeth, strange eyes, and the rest."

"We were going to tell you."

Pete cringed and wished Raine hadn't brought that subject up. "When the time was right."

"I get that. But I'm telling you now. The right time would've been before we had sex."

He almost chuckled. If he turned around, would he see a smile on her face? But he didn't risk it. Instead, he kept walking, giving her the time she needed.

* * * *

Unable to sleep, Callie had waited for the morning to come inside the cabin where she'd had sex with the Deacon brothers. But now that the time had arrived, she wished that the morning had never come.

She stood off to the side as the men faced The Council and attempted to stay calm. But it was hard when so many people were against her. The hard glares of The Council aimed at the Deacon brothers were nothing compared to the angry looks the rest of the people sent her way.

The clamor of everyone talking to their neighbor came to a stop as Charlton slammed his hand on the table in front of The Council members. "Come to order. We're here to decide what to do about the situation the Deacon brothers and their woman have put us in."

Their woman. No matter what had happened, she couldn't deny that those two words gave her a thrill. She raised her hand, not knowing what the proper etiquette was. "It's not their fault. I was the one who made friends with Scrunch."

Laughter as well as curses broke out around her and Charlton lifted a white eyebrow. "You can't make friends with one of The Cursed."

"I don't mean to be argumentative, but yes, you can. I did."

Tina waved her hand in the air, dismissing her statement and quieting the crowd. "It doesn't matter what she thinks she's done. Only what has happened matters."

Callie had liked Tina with her big smile and beautiful silver eyes when she'd run into her earlier that morning as Luke had escorted her to the cabin where The Council met, but now she couldn't help but feel like the tiny fairy was out to get her.

"I don't know if Scrunch is different from the rest or not, but he's trying to connect with me. Each time I've seen him, he hasn't shown any indication that he wanted to do me any harm."

She looked around her. Most of the others' expressions hadn't changed. They couldn't forget their past with The Cursed. Yet a few people, mainly the younger ones, leaned forward, wanting to hear more.

"What if they're trying to change? What if Scrunch is the first of more to come? What harm can it do to try?"

A small woman, her golden hair in curls around her head, stood and spoke. "I don't know if what she says is true, but if it is, then shouldn't we give it a chance? Maybe Callie and this Scrunch are the ones to finally make peace between us? I, for one, would love to live in a world where we didn't have to fear The Cursed."

A clamor rose then, with disagreement ringing out loud and clear. Yet a few of the others remained quiet, their silence giving her hope.

Charlton lifted his hand, signaling them to stop talking. "Whether

The Cursed are attempting to make contact is a question for another day."

Xnax bounced a fire ball in his hand then made it disappear in a puff of smoke. "As usual, Charlton is correct. We have to decide what to do about their breaking our rules. Not only did they allow her to take up with the creature—"

"No. They didn't allow me. No one *allows* me to do what I want to do. Contrary to what everyone might think, I'm not their captive and I don't take orders from them. I did this all on my own."

Why weren't the Deacon brothers sticking up for themselves? Instead, they stood straight and tall, their hands by their sides, mutely waiting for whatever decision came down.

Xnax conjured another ball and tossed it her way. Fortunately, it fell a few feet short of her. "If I can finish my statement..."

He paused as she nodded her head. Maybe she was doing them more harm by opening her big yap.

"The Deacon brothers also fought our own kind to protect her and the creature."

Another round of noise came from the spectators as they expressed their displeasure.

Charlton lifted his hand again and everyone quieted down. "We've never faced this situation before, but I think our choices are clear."

She swallowed, dread stiffening her spine. Would they make her leave? The thought of never seeing the men was awful. Could she leave if they made her? Yet, as much as she wanted to see the world away from the mountains, she wanted her men more.

She'd thought about it long and hard during the night. At first, she was sure she'd leave, sure that she had no place in their world, but when she imagined a life without the men, she'd broken down and cried. But would they let her stay now that she wanted to? Could she love men who could change into wolves? And yet a part of her reveled at the thought.

"Our first choice is that of banishment."

Callie sucked in a hard breath. *For me? Or for the men I love?*

She wavered, the world suddenly spinning. *Oh, hell. I love them so much. Please don't punish them for my actions.*

"The Deacon brothers will leave The Hidden and take Callie with them, never to return."

She couldn't, wouldn't let that happen even if it meant giving them up for good. "No. That's not fair. I dragged them into this trouble. Make me leave, but let them stay. Please don't take away their home. This is all my fault. Don't punish them. Punish me."

Was it her imagination, or did a couple of The Council members' faces appear to soften?

"The other option is to forgive their transgressions. However, Callie would have to promise to never have anything to do with The Cursed or this Scrunch creature ever again."

She nodded at Charlton, encouraging him to choose the second option. But if she stayed, could she keep the promise?

"Please," she whispered and fought back the tears. If she'd cost the men their sanctuary, their home, she'd never forgive herself.

Blue glanced her way, one of the few times he had since she'd arrived at the cabin. "We'll accept whatever decision you make as long as we're with Callie. We can't and we won't ever leave her."

Her heart opened wide, accepting the men in whatever form they came in. She wanted the proud, strong men standing up for her and she'd do whatever it took to protect them just as they'd protected her.

Charlton leaned his elbows on the table. "Very well then, let us vote. Xnax?"

Xnax bowed his head and when he lifted it, the hard tone of his face tightened the knot growing in her stomach. "Banishment for all of them."

She moved then, coming to Raine's side. "I'm so—"

Raine touched his finger to her lips, stilling her. "No. You don't have to say you're sorry. We did what we had to do and we'd do it again. As long as we end up together, we'll be happy."

She choked back a sob as she saw that Blue and Pete felt the same way. Instead, she lifted her head high and waited for the rest of the vote.

"Harrison?" asked Charlton.

"They turned on their own kind. As a werewolf, that's their worst crime." His eyes blazed with amber. "I vote for banishment."

"Tina?"

Callie gritted her teeth and prepared to hear the awful word again.

Tina found her gaze and held it. "I vote for forgiveness." The fairy smiled at her, letting her know that she'd already forgiven her.

"Wisa, what do you say?"

Wisa, whose face reminded Callie of an alley cat she'd once had, squared off with Charlton. "I vote for forgiveness also. After all, who amongst us hasn't made a mistake?"

Everyone turned their focus to Charlton. Callie gripped Raine's hand tighter.

"Very well." Charlton sighed. "That's two votes for banishment and two for forgiveness. Unhappily, that leaves the deciding vote up to me."

Charlton stood, preparing to cast his vote and proclaim the decision final. "I vote to—"

"Please, help me!"

As a group, they faced the frantic woman who'd flung the door wide and burst into the cabin. Her hair was as wild as her huge eyes. She pushed through the crowd that parted for her and reached for Charlton. Clutching his hand, she begged for help. "Please, The Cursed took my child. Please. Someone please help me."

Chapter Eight

Stunned at the woman's sudden appearance, Callie couldn't move, but that didn't keep several men, including the Deacon brothers, from coming to her side.

"Shelly, slow down. Tell us what happened." Blue took the young woman by the arms and gently shook her.

Tears streamed down her face and her body shook as she tried to tell them what had happened to her child. "The Cursed took her. My little Bryna was playing by the woods near the path leading to the waterfall. I swear I only took my eyes off her for a second and then, when I looked back, I saw one of them put his hand over her mouth and pull her into the bushes. I screamed then ran after them, but I couldn't find her."

She fell against Blue's chest and he had to wrap his arms around her to keep her on her feet. "Please, she's all I have. Please find my little girl."

Callie's heart went out to Shelly. The worst thing she could think of, even more than having to give up the men she loved, was to lose a child. But she had to wonder. Why would The Cursed want the girl? No matter what everyone had told her about them, she couldn't think of Scrunch as an evil creature. If his kind would take a child, then why hadn't he hurt her?

"We will. I promise you we will." Blue handed the woman off to Lyra who stood nearby, then waved for the other men to follow him.

"I'll bet that damn creature Callie was messing with is behind this."

She gaped at Harrison. "You don't know that."

He lifted his lip in a snarl. "And you don't know it didn't. They're all alike. Murdering animals is all they are."

"No. Not Scrunch." She answered the crowd's glares with one of her own. "And I'll bet more of them are like him."

"Let's go. I know where their cave is."

Pete and Raine were among the men who followed Blue out of the cabin. The other people in the camp shouted at them to bring the child back and to make The Cursed pay for what they did.

Could Scrunch have done this?

She could be wrong in not accepting the perception of him that the others had, but her gut told her differently. Just like her intuition had told her that she needn't be afraid of the Deacon men, it told her that Scrunch was not a part of the kidnapping. Maybe one of his people had taken the girl, but she couldn't let Scrunch take the blame.

To prove they were wrong, she dashed after them.

The throng of ten people surged down the mountain like a steamroller, moving everyone out of their way. Even though she expected them to go to the path that led to the water, Blue took them to the opposite side of the camp and broke through the trees.

Still behind the rest, she picked up her speed. But it didn't help. A painful stitch in her side threatened to stop her, but she pushed on.

Then, without warning, a surge of energy hit her, invigorating her. Like the time before, she could sense the presence of something else inside her, almost as though another part of her, one that had lain dormant for years, had come to life. The colors of the world around her dimmed into a mist of amber, but she could see things sharper than ever before. Even as she hurried to stay up with the others, she picked up the soft sounds of animals ducking for cover and quivering in fear.

Was it adrenaline that gave her renewed energy and infused her body with strength?

They charged through the forest, passing the hole where she and Scrunch had first met and continuing on for several long minutes. Just as she was starting to wonder if she could keep up, the group came to a stop at Blue's order.

"There it is."

She pushed through the crowd, receiving a few hard nudges along the way, and came to Blue's side. "They live in that cave?"

The small opening in the mountain was barely large enough to fit three men, shoulder to shoulder, across it. "Are you sure? It's so small."

"Yeah, I'm sure."

"Watch out."

She glanced at Pete who stood, along with Raine, behind their brother, then followed his gaze to the cave. A group of animals all like Scrunch spilled from the entrance. Their red eyes blazed and their snarls showed their fangs.

Where's Scrunch?

She scanned the group of black animals, their hands dragging on the ground, as they growled and paced back and forth in front of the cave. They weren't attacking, but it was evident that they weren't about to run, either.

"Where's the little girl?" The man who'd asked the question moved from the middle of the group to the front. "We're going to have to go in and get her."

"There she is. There's my little girl."

Shelly appeared out of the crowd and started running toward The Cursed. Blue was right behind her and grabbed her, pulling her away from them.

"Mommy!"

Bryna's dress was dirty, but she appeared uninjured. One of creatures held her arm, and even from a distance, Callie could see how his fingers sank into her flesh. He hadn't broken the skin yet since there was no blood, but if he gripped her any harder, he would.

Shelly struggled to get free, but Blue held her long enough to pass her off to one of the other men. She cried out for Bryna, who answered with pleas for help.

Blue's face was emotionless and that frightened Callie more than anything else. "Everyone spread out. This is going to be rough."

He turned to her. "Callie, when the fighting starts, see if you can grab her. If you can, don't hang around. Get back to camp as fast as you can." He pivoted to the men and began talking in hushed tones about their best plan of attack.

Scrunch caught her eye. He stood on the outside of his people, his diamond patch brilliant white against the mass of black. He held his hand in the air in a salute. Or at least that's what she hoped it was.

Moving as quietly as she could, Callie slipped away from the group. Then, when she was sure she was far enough away that even one of the men couldn't catch her, she took off running.

"Callie!"

Pete was the first to spot her, but it was too late to catch her. She ran as hard as she could, picking up the adrenaline she'd felt before, until she skidded to a few feet in front of the throng of The Cursed. She could hear the angry and fearful cries of those behind her.

"Stay back, Pete. And keep the others in check. I can do this."

She lifted her hand as Scrunch had done. He skirted around the edge of his group, earning snarls from a few of his kind, then drew within a yard of her.

"Tell your people to give her back." She pivoted to face him, but kept glancing at the girl, trying to make her meaning clear. "Please, you have to understand."

He grunted, but his gaze whipped to Bryna before settling on her again. Another grunt came, but she was no closer to understanding him than before.

She pointed at Bryna. The bigger creature that held her snarled and dragged her closer to Callie. But she didn't dare hope that he knew what she wanted. Instead, she pleaded with Scrunch again and pointed at the child.

"Let her go."

Scrunch tilted his head to the side.

At least he's trying to understand.

"Callie, move very slowly and get away from them."

She called to Blue, trying to comfort him. "I know what I'm doing. Just don't make any sudden moves. We don't want to spook them."

Taking a deep breath that she hoped wasn't her last, she turned on her heel and started walking toward the child and her captor. He growled, his intent unmistakable, but she wouldn't give up.

Amazing herself, she got close enough to see the growing amber in Bryna's eyes. The amber was bright with fear.

"It's okay, sweetie. They won't hurt you."

"I want my mommy," she whimpered.

"I know and she's here. Just hang on a little while longer." She reached out and took the child's other arm.

The creature's growl grew louder, sending chills down her spine. She held her ground and kept her head high. "Give her to me."

Another growl told her he wouldn't. She craned her neck around to find Scrunch. "Get him to give her to me. Please."

Scrunch's eyes narrowed a second before he let out a screech and pointed behind her. Callie twisted back to the child and the larger creature in time to see him toss Bryna to the ground and throw himself at her. Stunned, she couldn't move, couldn't get away. Scrunch flew past her, knocking her out of the way and to the ground beside the girl.

"Run." She pushed Bryna onto her feet. Pete grabbed Bryna once she'd made it halfway back to their group. Blue and Raine dashed toward Callie and, taking her under each arm, helped her up. They half carried, half pulled her to safety.

Growls and snarls filled her ears and she tried to see what was happening, but the men wouldn't let her turn around. They continued to carry her along with the crowd as everyone rushed back to camp.

"Keep moving, everyone."

"Are they after us?" cried one woman.

Pete carried Bryna with her mother running at his side. Callie groaned as Raine, lifting her like she weighed nothing, cradled her in his arms.

The sound of many feet thundered in the forest as they ran and soon the noise of fighting amongst the creatures was lost. Raine, his heart pounding against her cheek, slowed to a stop. "Are you trying to get yourself killed?"

But she couldn't answer. Her body had no strength to move. Instead, she closed her eyes and let the tears fall.

* * * *

Blue studied Callie lying on the quilts in their tent. He'd experienced fear before, but nothing had compared to what he'd felt when the creature had flung itself at her. She'd fallen asleep after Raine had taken her into his arms, and ignoring the call of The Council to bring her in front of them, they'd taken her to their tent. Charlton's decision could wait.

But Charlton had other ideas. Instead, he'd summoned Blue to come to him as soon as possible. Blue had done so, expecting the worst.

"She's waking up." Pete leaned over her and dabbed a moist cloth to her forehead.

Her eyelids fluttered until, at last, she opened her beautiful brown eyes. She stretched and shot them a smile.

"Hey, you. It's about time you came around."

She blinked, then sat up. "Is she all right? Did Bryna get scratched?"

He could smell her relief. "No. She was lucky. She came out of it unharmed, but with the realization that she shouldn't play alone by the woods."

Blue knelt beside her along with his brothers. "Charlton

summoned me so he could tell me the decision. He cast his vote."

She took his hand. "Let me talk to him and make him understand. I'll leave, but he can't throw you out of your home. It's not fair." She tried to get up, but he eased her back down.

"Calm down. It's okay. He voted for forgiveness."

"No way."

He grinned at her choice of words and answered in kind. "Yes way. But there's more."

"Do I want to know what that is?"

Pete slid his hand along her hair, smoothing it to her back. "Maybe. Do you remember how you came here? Do you remember what happened when the buck chased you?"

"Of course I do. I fell into a huge hole. A girl tends to remember that kind of thing."

"What my brother is trying to get at is this. You said you felt this weird kind of sensation, like walking through invisible water."

"Uh-huh." She pulled her knees to her chest. "And?"

"To get into The Hidden, someone has to be a supernatural being. Or touch one as they enter."

"But I'm human and I wasn't touching anyone."

"We know you were alone." Blue took over. "Which means you must be a supernatural. Or at least be a descendant of one. Otherwise, you never could have gotten inside. We think what you went through must be a new portal that's opened up. It's too soon to know much, but The Council has sent a group to study it."

Pete chimed in. "They'll study and guard it in case others wander through."

"I still don't understand. You think an ancestor of mine is a supernatural being?"

She was having a difficult time understanding what he meant, so he had to make it clearer. "The Council and we believe you're part werewolf."

She refused it. "No, I would've known, wouldn't I? And why a werewolf? How do you know I'm not the descendant of a fairy or a troll?"

"No troll ever looked like you and you're too tall to be a fairy. We don't know for certain, but, after seeing your eyes change—"

She gripped Blue's arm. "My eyes changed? How? When?"

"I saw your eyes a moment before you decided to play heroine. They were filled with amber."

"Which means I'm part werewolf." She trembled and ducked her head.

Was she upset to find out? Would she embrace her inner wolf or hate knowing that it existed? "What are you thinking, Callie?"

She lifted her head. Her mouth was parted, making him ache to press his lips to hers.

"I'm not sure. But how could I not have known?"

"I can't answer that. Sometimes people who have werewolf blood never realize it until they meet another werewolf. Or, like you, their wolf side attempts to break through in a time of extreme emotion, like fear."

"And you're sure about this?"

"Yeah. We are. There's no denying that color in your eyes."

"I'm part werewolf. Wow."

Blue had wanted to wait to ask her. He and his brothers had wanted to give her more time, but Charlton was forcing their hand. "There's more."

Her draw dropped open. "You've got to be kidding me. What more could there be?"

"Charlton voted for forgiveness only if you promise to do what he asks."

She was up and on her feet, moving to the other side of the tent. If he wasn't already sure, he would've known from her improved speed that her werewolf side was growing stronger.

"What is it with you people and your promises?"

"He voted for forgiveness if you promise to stay in The Hidden."

* * * *

Callie's heart raced as she crossed the room and ended up in the middle of their quilt bed. "Then you can tell Charlton and the rest of The Council that…"

The men shifted on their feet and stared at her. Blue ran a hand over his face and blew out a slow breath. "Be careful. Think about what you're going to say."

"Pff. You act like I'm going to tell the old coot—"

"Callie, no." Pete grimaced and stalked away. "Watch your mouth. We're in a tent, you know. It's not exactly soundproof."

"As I was going to say, you can tell *Charlton* that I accept. But—"

The men were on her with Raine lifting her off her feet and swinging her around. "Are you serious?"

"Don't question it, bro." Pete pulled her away from his brother and swung her around again. "We wouldn't want her to change her mind."

When Pete put her down, Blue turned her around and confronted her. "Go on. What were you going to say?"

"I was going to say that'll I stay if you three will make not one, but two promises to me." She bit her lip, dying to tell them, but wanting to play the game.

"Anything. Whatever you want, whatever you need us to do, we promise. Right, guys?" Pete slapped Raine on the shoulder as his brother nodded before he'd even finished speaking.

"Hold up. I'd like to know what I'm promising before I say yes or no to it." Blue tilted his head and waited. "Well?"

She paced a few feet away, needing the distance to hold back her surging desire to pull their bodies closer. "The first promise is this. I want you to make me your mate."

"Are you saying that you love us, Callie?"

She rolled her eyes at Blue. "Answer me first. Do you love me enough to make me your mate?"

"Done!" exclaimed Raine. Again, Pete was in total agreement.

Blue's brow knitted in a frown. "Do you really understand what that means?"

"If you mean that I'll change into a werewolf, then yes, I do. But I'm already part werewolf, so what's the big deal?" Didn't he still want her? Or was he trying to get out of a relationship that had barely started?

"That's not the same as being a full werewolf. You may have experienced some of the effects, like the change in eye color, but shifting into your wolf form is a whole other matter. It hurts, especially the first few times."

She jutted out her chin. "So you don't think I can handle it?"

She'd gotten to him. She could see it in the way his mouth curved up at the ends.

"It's not that. But what about the rest? You'll have to give up your life on The Outside. Yes, you can visit, but you'll live here with us." He swept his arm around the room. "Here. Without modern conveniences and everything else that you're used to."

"You mean like guns and pollution and the rest of it? Yeah, I think I can do without a microwave for a life in Shangri-La." She came near him, needing to touch him, to feel the way his body reacted to hers. She skimmed her fingers along his arm and felt him tremble.

"What other obstacles do you have in mind, Mr. Deacon? Or don't you want me anymore?"

He jerked back, stunned at her question. "I want you more than life itself. I love you, Callie. Even with all the trouble you've caused."

"Me? I haven't done anything except try to bring peace to this place." She placed her palm against his cheek and loved how the bristles of his beard tickled her skin. "But that brings me to the other promise."

Pete slid behind her and pulled her ass to his crotch. "Tell us."

She crooked her finger at Raine to bring him closer. "I want you to help me bring peace between your people." She grinned and added, "Between *our* people and The Cursed."

They broke away from her at the same time, leaving her heart and body bereft. She hadn't expected them to like the idea, but she hadn't thought they'd react in such an extreme fashion.

"Come on, guys. Can't you see that it's possible after what happened with Scrunch? He protected me against his own kind. Doesn't that show that he's not an evil creature?"

"No. All that shows is that you were able to train him like a pet. And pets often protect their masters."

Was Blue that resistant? "Look, that's what I'm going to do if I stay here. I'm not going to spend my days tending to your needs like some 1950s wilderness wife. I want to make a difference, and with your help, I can."

"You'll be breaking your promise to Charlton."

"I know and I'm willing to risk it." She turned to face Pete and Raine. "Will you two help me even if Blue doesn't? If you want to say no, I'll understand."

They both glanced at their older brother before Pete took a step forward. "To have you stay? To have you be our mate? Then yeah, I'll help you no matter what Charlton and the rest say. It's time for a change around here."

Raine joined him. "Me, too. I think maybe you're right. Scrunch did protect you. A few of the others saw what he did, too. So maybe there is a chance. If there is then, yes, I'll help, just as long as you stay safe while playing ambassador to The Cursed. No more running off in the middle of the night, okay?"

She placed a hand on each of their arms. "Deal." Turning, she held her breath, not asking, but simply waiting for Blue to take his stand.

"Come on, bro," urged Pete.

She saw his resolve waver in the blink of his eyes and in the way his body relaxed. "Blue?"

"Fine. We'll give it a try, but that's all I'm promising."

She squealed with delight and spun in a circle. "Great. Then let's do this. Do you want to change me now or later?"

Blue grabbed her and held her to him. His eyes blazed with amber and his scent overwhelmed her. Her knees felt weak, but she knew he wasn't about to let her fall. At least not until he laid her down on the quilt.

"We can do it now, but claiming a mate is usually done after The Pledging Ceremony."

"What's The Pledging Ceremony?"

Pete lifted a carafe of dark liquid from a nearby shelf. "It's a ceremony where we pledge our love to you and you to us. Then the rest of the community accepts you as one of us."

Raine held up two goblets while Pete filled them. He passed one to Blue and one to her, then got two more for Pete to fill. "Should I tell Charlton that we want the ceremony as soon as possible?"

"There's nothing I want more. Still…"

"Still what? Are you changing your mind?"

"Not on your life. But a lot of the people here aren't very happy with me right now."

She hated to think of that, but it had to be said. She lifted the goblet to her mouth and took a sip. The wine, unlike any she'd ever tasted, caressed her throat and made her dizzy. "Maybe a private ceremony would be better."

Blue brought his goblet to his mouth, then wiped his lips. "She's right. Charlton can do the honors right here. Pete, go ask him if he can do it right now."

Her nerves came to life, making her doubt her chances. "Are you sure he'll do it? What if he doesn't want to? What if he wants me to stay, but he doesn't think I'm good enough for you?"

Blue cupped her by the neck and crushed a kiss to her lips. The intensity, the possessiveness of the kiss sent her head swimming more than any drink ever could. She was breathless by the time he turned her loose.

"Whatever happens, we'll always be with you."

Chapter Nine

"For a minute, I thought he was going to crucify me instead of pledging me to you." Callie lay against the quilt, naked and ready for her men to make her theirs for the rest of her life.

"He didn't look pleased, but, since you did what he wanted, then he couldn't say much against it. Besides, he did join us. That alone shows he wants you to stay."

The Pledging Ceremony had been brief but beautiful as the men had spoken words of endearment, vowing to love her forever. She'd done the same, fighting back tears. It had only been Charlton along with Titto to witness their joining, but it had been enough. The thing that mattered was that she was now their mate.

Blue lounged beside her on one side with Raine joining them near her feet. She studied Pete as he strode around their tent lighting candles, and enjoyed the way his muscles flexed. He was a perfect man just like her other two men were.

My men. Wow.

"Pete, are you coming or what?"

"Just a minute." He moved to the next candle and lit it.

"Do you think the others will accept me in time?" What would she do if they didn't? Once the others found out that she wanted peace with Scrunch's people, who knew what they'd think?

"They will. Once they get to know you better." Raine trailed his fingers along her side then over the crevice between her leg and her torso to twist his fingers in the curly hair of her mound.

She groaned and shoved against Blue's shoulder. What was taking them so long to make love to her? What about changing her into a full werewolf?

"Until then, we get you all to ourselves." Blue pushed her hand away, then leaned over to snag her nipple between his teeth.

Opening her legs, Callie shoved on him again, urging him to go lower, and he didn't hesitate, muttering words of joy as he slid his arms under her legs and pulled them on top of his shoulders.

Raine groaned and took his finger to move her pussy lips apart. "Blue, taste her, man. I want to watch you enjoy her juices."

"You don't have to tell me again." Blue crushed his mouth to her pussy, found her tender clit, and flicked his tongue over it.

Callie groaned, and called Pete to her side. His cock pointed straight at her face and she took his cock, the heat from it warming her hand as she tightened it around Pete's shaft. She pulled him to her mouth and sucked, matching Blue's rhythm as he showed her just how hungry he was for her taste. Pre-cum filled her mouth and she mewled, telling him that she, too, was enjoying herself.

She let the sensations wash over her, thrilling her. Her pussy clenched, throbbing, pulsing as her body readied for the delicious end. Her heart thundered in her ears and her pulse sped up. She breathed in deeply, catching each man's unique aroma to tingle in her nostrils.

Blue licked her clit, using his teeth to nibble and send stabs of quick pain. Raine found the crevice between her leg and stomach, and feathered kisses along her skin to tantalize and tempt her. She reached for him, but he stayed just out of her touch. She opened her legs wider, giving both men silent encouragement.

She cupped Pete's balls then slid her hands farther along to find his butt cheek. Not having room to spank him as he'd done the last time they were together, she dug her fingers into his butt cheek.

"Take it easy, girl. Don't rake the skin off." He took her breast and squeezed it, giving her a little taste of her own actions. In retaliation, she sucked his cock farther inside then let it slip out with her teeth skimming over his loose skin.

The first of many orgasms rumbled through her body, sending

stars to flash behind her eyes. She pumped Pete's dick harder. His tender skin moved under her palm, sliding against her flesh like water flowing over her hand. She moaned and put her hand over Pete's and pressed down. She wanted him to punish her breasts again, but with his teeth next time. He pulled her arm from between his legs and brushed her hand away from her breast. His tongue lashed her taut nipple and she arched, wanting him to give both breasts attention.

Releasing Pete's cock, she cried out in ecstasy as Blue spanked the side of her thigh. Sliding his finger between her butt cheeks, he worked the tight muscles of her ass, probing, exploring, then moaning his excitement when she constricted her muscles to capture his finger.

He sucked on her clit, using his tongue to enter her pussy, and drove his finger deeper into her butt hole. She clenched her muscles, and tried to take both his tongue and his finger.

Their eyes mesmerized her, with amber flecks growing to overtake their normal color. Their faces were tight with concentration, their jaws locked in determination to hold back their climaxes. She blinked and stared at Raine.

Are those fangs sticking out over his lower lip?

He glanced at her and smiled, opening his mouth to let her see the fangs more. She shook her head, and the fangs receded.

Werewolves.

They'd told her what they were, and aside from Raine, she'd seen them in their alter-forms, but even now she was having a tough time wrapping her mind around the truth. Yet the strangest thing wasn't that. Instead, the fact that it didn't bother her, but in fact, thrilled her, was even odder.

She sighed, but the sigh was muffled as Pete kissed her hard, then turned her loose. She opened her eyes to find him staring at her, an expression of love softening his features.

"Hey, baby."

She pretended to be angry and showed it with her look.

He laughed. "I know. You don't like that nickname."

"Did we ever decide on which name to use?" asked Raine. "Aside from *ours*, that is?"

"Use my name."

Blue lifted his head from between her legs. "You're ours, all right, and that's the way it is. We captured you and we'll give you the name we like. Got it?"

She started to respond, but lost her ability to speak as Pete nibbled on her ear and Blue resumed his fervent attack on her clit. Desire rolled through her like a rocket through space, unimpeded by any obstacle. She cried out as a climax ripped her apart.

Pete lowered his mouth to her tit and licked her nipple much the same way Blue was lapping up her cum. She latched onto Pete's cock again and started pumping. Somehow she managed to hold on as Blue coaxed another orgasm out of her.

Blue drank her juices then rose and wiped his mouth. "Damn, but she tastes good."

Raine's finger slid over her mons to stroke her. "Fuck her, Blue."

"Yeah, Blue. Take her from the front while I take her ass." Raine pushed on her thigh and she turned onto her side, letting Pete's cock pop from her mouth. "I'll use her juices to get her ready."

Pete grumbled, then positioned himself for her to take him again. He lifted her head to meet his cock and she swallowed him, closing her mouth over his mushroomed tip. He groaned and tunneled his hand through her hair. She wrapped her hand around the base of him and pumped hard, bringing him in and out in quick movements.

Blue positioned his cock at her pussy then shoved inside her pussy at the same moment he whacked her thigh. She yelped, but the sound was muffled by Pete's cock in her mouth.

Her heart raced as Pete put his cock into her butt hole. After spreading some of her juices along with his pre-cum in and over her anal muscles, he hadn't eased into her, but shoved his cock in, giving her no time to prepare for him. But it didn't matter. She loved the way his cock pushed against her anal walls, loved the friction his forceful action gave her. After the first brief stab of pain, she no longer cared. She moved back and forth, one man entering her as the other left.

A storm of immeasurable power coursed through her pussy and ass then joined together in her abdomen. The musky taste of Pete mixed with the scent of Raine's breath as he leaned over to nibble on her shoulder. His crotch bumped her butt cheeks. In between thrusts, he added a pinch or a slap to her sensitive butt.

Pete teased both her nipples, shooting little zings of delightful pain to add to the delightful friction coming from both her pussy and her butt. Her blood pounded in her ears and her body stiffened, drawing ever closer to the final release.

They gave her their bodies as they'd already given her their hearts. She trembled, not from the sexual pleasures but from the realization that she'd found the men that would love her forever. And in finding her men, she'd found her first real home.

Yet another orgasm, the strongest so far, broke free and she gripped the bed, clutching the quilt.

The scent of them filled her head and made her dizzy with desire as strong as when they'd first touched her. The sounds of the men enjoying her, their groans and grunts echoing in the small room, gave her another burst of lust to heighten the sensation of three pairs of hands exploring her body. Pete straightened up, then shot his wad. She swallowed as fast as she could, but she couldn't drink it all. Some of it ran down her cheek to the quilt below.

"Ahhhhhh. Drink me."

Pete's body jerked in spams of his climax, then he pulled out as the last of it spilled from him. Once he had recovered, he grabbed another pillowcase and wiped her mouth. She licked what she could from her lips as he cleaned her.

She spoke in broken breaths. "Say it again."

"Say what again?" Raine spanked her butt again. "Damn, it's a rush to see your flesh ripple under my hand."

"Call me the nickname you want."

Blue shoved his cock inside her, then shoved into her again. "Ours."

The word *ours* had never sounded so right.

Blue thrust into her time and time again as Raine slapped her thigh and pumped his cock past the constricting rings of her anal muscles. Blue, his eyes closed and his face set, gripped her leg hard and groaned a second before he released. He quivered, holding onto her, until at last, he groaned and fell away from her.

Raine followed him a moment later, shouting his release. The men slumped beside her as they all worked to bring their breathing back to normal.

"Callie, you're more than we hoped for. Hell, I don't think we even dared to dream for someone as wonderful as you. We love you."

Blue and Pete echoed his words. "We love you."

Blue slid his hand across her stomach to cup her breast. Pete, on the other side of her, played with a strand of her hair.

Surrounded by her men, Callie reveled in her new role as their mate, the one woman they wanted in their lives. She laughed, loving how fate had brought them together.

"You're ours."

Funny, how she loved hearing that word now.

Fondling her breast, Pete nibbled on her ear, then licked her shoulder and whispered his love for her in her ear. Raine traced circles around her other nipple as Blue moved to the end of the bed.

"Now that I've been pledged to you, don't you think it's about time you changed me?"

"Not until we hear you say you love us, too." Raine flicked his tongue over her nipple.

Had she really not told them? "I love you. Raine, Blue, and Pete, I love you with everything I am." She adopted an excited expression. "Now make me a werewolf. Or, maybe I should say, make me more of a werewolf."

"Are you sure you're ready?" Blue edged nearer.

"You bet I am." She sat up, bringing them along with her as they crowded around her. "What do I have to do?"

They changed, the amber in their eyes flashing as their fangs slid over their lower lips. Raine took her hand and licked it, then gripped her chin, making her look at him. "The only thing you have to do is remember that we love you. That will get you through the pain and to the other side."

Alarm threatened to take her, to make her change her mind, but she held fast, ready for whatever torture might lie ahead. "Do it."

She screamed as three sets of fangs dug into her skin, one on each shoulder with Raine driving his teeth into her arm. Instinct took over and she fought against them, but they kept her as still as they could. She screamed again as the pain fired outward from each wound. Her body shook and her eyes rolled back in her head. Darkness took her as her scream turned into a whimper.

* * * *

The wind blew through Callie's fur and into her open mouth as she raced along the ridge with her wolves. The world around her was amber-hued and her keen eyesight and sense of smell picked up sights and aromas she'd never known existed before she'd gone through the first transformation.

Hearing their paws pounding into the ground, she sped up, determined to make them earn the position at the head of the pack. She had no doubt they would, as they always did, trading the leader's spot throughout the night. She led the pack for now, but that wouldn't last long. Blue hated taking a position behind her.

She'd awakened after they'd bitten her to find the world a different place. The wolf she'd sensed inside her, yet had never recognized it for what it was, roared to life, ready to show her a world she could never have dreamed of. Her inner wolf had made the transition easier than it would've been if she'd been entirely human.

Since that day, she'd changed many times and now she could do so as fast as her men could.

A nip on her butt sent her flying faster, almost stumbling over her feet as she tried to outpace them. Blue charged up to run beside her, his tongue lolling out of his mouth, his ears preened forward to catch any unusual sound. Raine and Pete joined her on the other side, their amber eyes glued on her. Her time to lead was at an end. At least for tonight.

Without warning, Raine threw his golden-furred body against hers, stopping their run. She spilled over him, both of them rolling a few feet before they finally came to a stop. She growled, flashing her teeth as she got back onto her feet.

Raine's warning growl turned her around to find Blue and Pete, their bodies tense, their heads lowered. Just beyond them stood six of The Cursed. The creatures showed their fangs and jostled back and forth, but didn't come any closer.

Raine joined his brothers, forming a defensive line in front of her. She padded forward even as Blue growled another warning. Although she tried to get past them, they nipped and snapped at her, keeping her behind them.

Her wolf's mind howled, scratching to tear The Cursed apart. But it was her human side that won out. Shifting back to human, she stood up and marched past the snarling wolves.

"Scrunch."

Scrunch eased to the front of his group. He tilted his head at her then whirled around to growl at his companions. They quieted, but still remained restless, their bodies twitching, their red eyes glowing.

"How are you, Scrunch? You're staying out of holes, like I'm doing, right?" She wished she had a piece of fruit to share with him.

Raine transformed into his human body. "Callie, be careful."

She didn't bother glancing at him. She could hear the worry in his voice. "It's okay. If they'd wanted to attack, they'd have already done it."

"Still…"

"I will. Don't worry."

She reached out her hand, palm up, toward Scrunch. Both groups reacted, jostling about with nervous energy.

"Callie, if he scratches you…"

"He won't."

Yet she still held her breath when he lifted his hand toward her. With his paw-like hand shaking with as much trepidation as she was feeling, he touched the tip of his finger to the middle of her palm. She smiled, mouth closed so he wouldn't take it as a threat.

One of The Cursed growled and Scrunch yanked his hand back. Surprised, she jerked her hand away, too. The Cursed backed away, keeping their faces toward her, then, once they were at a distance, they whirled around and disappeared into the forest line.

Raine grabbed her and held her tightly. "Hell, don't ever do that again. I think I lost ten years off my life."

"But it worked, don't you see?" Her body hummed with excitement. "We made contact with The Cursed and no one got hurt on either side."

"You're lucky they didn't attack us. We were outnumbered." Raine's blue eyes sparkled as his brothers, still in wolf form, paced around them, growling their displeasure.

"But they didn't. That proves we have a chance of making peace."

"Maybe. But let's try keeping them at a distance for a while."

"Aw, where's the fun in that?"

"Look, woman, don't make us have to tie you up again."

She touched his face, tenderly. "And treat me like your captive?"

"If we have to." He brushed the hair away from her face.

"Then go ahead. Tie me up."

"Yeah?"

She pulled out of his arms and stepped back. "Yeah. Why not? It's just my body. You captured my heart the first time I looked at you."

With a wink and a toss of her hair, she let the transformation take her again. A few moments later, she spun off to the right and dashed down the hillside. She sported a wolfish grin as her men followed behind her, once more vying for the lead.

THE END

WWW.JANEJAMISON.COM

ABOUT THE AUTHOR

Jane Jamison has always liked "weird stuff," as her mother called it. From an early age she was fascinated with stories about werewolves, vampires, space, aliens, and whatever was hiding in her bedroom closet. (To this day, she still swears she can hear growls and moans whenever the lights are out.)

Being born under the sign of Scorpio meant Jane was destined to be very sensual. Some would say she was (and remains) downright sexual. Then one day she put her two favorite things together on paper and found her life's true ambition: to be an erotic paranormal romance author.

Jane spends at least six days a week locked in her office surrounded by the characters she loves. Every day a new character will knock on the door of her imagination. Her plans include taking care of her loving husband, traveling, and writing at least twelve books a year.

For all titles by Jane Jamison, please visit
www.bookstrand.com/jane-jamison

Siren Publishing, Inc.
www.SirenPublishing.com

CPSIA information can be obtained at www.ICGtesting.com
Printed in the USA
LVOW10s0056270216

476943LV00028B/310/P